A BOY AT WAR

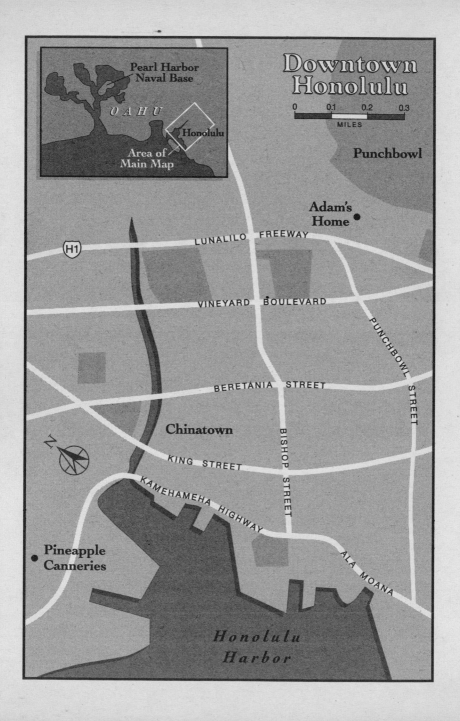

A BOY AT WAR

A Novel of
Pearl Harbor

HARRY MAZER

SCHOLASTIC INC.

New York Toronto London Auckland Sydney
Mexico City New Delhi Hong Kong Buenos Aires

ISBN 0-439-35207-X

12 11 10 9 8 7 6 5 4   1 2 3 4 5 6/0

Printed in the U.S.A.   40

First Scholastic printing, September 2001

Cover design by Paul Zakris and Mark Siegel
Book design by Paul Zakris
The text for this book is set in 11-point Janson.

FOR MY SON, JOE

ACKNOWLEDGMENTS

My thanks to Mary Pope Osborne and Ron Savage for sharing their memories of growing up in the military, and to Solomon Kaulukukui, Jr., for his patience and good humor in unfailingly responding to my many queries about Hawaiian life.

Nobody, however young, returns from war still a boy.

—SAMUEL HYNES, *Flights of Passage: Reflections of a WWII Aviator*

1

"Drop me off here, Mom," Adam said. They were a couple of blocks from the school.

"Why? I don't mind driving."

"Mom!" He couldn't control his impatience. "This is high school." Bad enough that he was registering late—it was already November and the term was half over. "Here," he said. "Drop me off here," and he hopped out of the car.

By the time he got everything straightened out in the office, his first-period class had started. The teacher was in the middle of a lesson. Adam stood in front of the class while Mr. Handler interrogated him.

"Where are you from, Adam?"

"No place," Adam said. He was trying to be accurate, but it came out sounding sullen.

"No place? I've never been to no place."

"I'm military," he explained.

"And where's that? Pearl Harbor? Hickman Field? Or is it Fort Knox?"

"America," Adam said, stiffly. "The United States of America."

He was sorry the minute he said it. It sounded so phony and superpatriotic, as if he were going to snap his heels together

ing in the corner of the room.
said. He fixed Adam with a dis-
Americans here," he instructed,
aii, are still only a territory of the
mericans, and we will be a state. Now,
. Your hometown, your place of origin,

a hometown. He'd grown up in the military,
and in the military you moved all the time. There was no one
place. They'd lived all over, but no matter where they lived, it
was always the same—military. Whatever you thought was a
military base, that was his hometown.

But it was too complicated to explain. Easier to say, "I'm
from Adams Center, New York." Which was not the truth,
but not a lie, either. His grandfather Pelko had a farm there,
and they visited him sometimes. Just before they got their
orders to Hawaii, they had been there.

"Adams Center, and your name is Adam? Are you pulling
my leg?" Mr. Handler said. "Are you trying to be comical?"

"No, sir." Adam had his eyes fixed on an empty seat in the
back of the room.

Mr. Handler went to the blackboard and pulled down a map
of the United States. "Show us where Adams Center is,
Adam."

He couldn't find it on the map, or the next biggest town,
Watertown, either. "It's not there." None of this was making
him look too bright. "It's a tiny place," he explained, and
pointed to Lake Ontario. "It's next to that."

"A tiny place next to a great lake," the teacher said. "How many Great Lakes are there, class? Who knows their names?"

Adam knew, but he was through answering questions.

A boy with his head on the desk raised his hand. "Davi?" Mr. Handler said. The boy sat up. He had a thatch of thick black hair and a muzzy look like he had just woken up.

Japanese or maybe Chinese, Adam thought, *something like that. Maybe Hawaiian.* He'd been reading about Hawaii. There were a lot of different kinds of people here—Chinese, Japanese, Filipinos, Portuguese—and they were all mixed up. There were more Japanese, though, than any other group.

"Five lakes," Davi said, showing five fingers, and reeled off their names, as if they were almost too boring to say. "Lake Ontario, Lake Erie, Lake Michigan, Lake Huron, Lake Superior."

"Sticky brain," someone said.

Davi looked around. "At least I have a brain."

"Class! Quiet. Adam, can you tell us something about Adams Center?"

Adam was on his way to the back of the room. "It snows a lot," he said.

On the road to Aiea it showered twice, and twice the rain clouds came streaming across the volcanic Koolau Mountains. Curtains of rain spilled down the steep slopes. Water sprayed up from the bike wheels. Adam thought of taking cover, but he was intent on getting to Aiea to see if his father's ship was back in port yet. He'd left on a training cruise ten days ago.

The rain stopped as fast as it had started. The sun came out, and Adam was dry in minutes. He was used to snow in November and never seeing the sun for days at a time, but this was Hawaii, where the sun shone even when it rained.

They'd only been there two weeks, but he liked it. He liked Hawaii. When you were a military brat, that was the drill. Whatever happened, you liked it. One year they'd moved four times so they could be with his father. Did he like it? Yeah, sure, he liked it.

"Join the Navy and See the World." That was what the posters promised, and it was true, because here they were in the middle of the Pacific Ocean, two thousand miles away from the United States, on the island of Oahu, in the city of Honolulu, next door to Pearl Harbor, the biggest American naval base in the Pacific.

He knew the facts, that was the easy part of moving. The

hard part was making new friends. And here, in Roosevelt High, for the first time he was in a civilian school with civilian kids. He'd already figured out that they didn't like military kids a whole lot. Well, okay. He got along anyway. He was good at sports, and he could give as well as take, so it wasn't as if he was by himself. What he missed, though, was having one good friend.

When he was younger, he had always gone to schools on the base, and all the kids were navy, like him. They knew about moving and the military, and how you didn't pal around with kids whose dads were lower in rank than yours. It wasn't a written rule, but it was a rule. The kids all lived by military rules, same as their fathers. They were in the military too, even if they didn't have the uniforms.

When Adam's father got home, he was going to ask Adam how he was getting along. And Adam was going to say what he always said: "Everything's super." His father had no use for complainers and whiners. He always said, "Adam, you've got to take the cards you're dealt. The important thing is how you play the game."

Kamehameha Highway was a hilly two-lane road all the way to Aiea. Adam rode his bike around to the back of the sugar mill, where he could see the whole harbor. He'd been here before, and he liked the view—the spread of the harbor, Ford Island in the middle, and beyond it, hills of green sugarcane, and beyond them, almost floating in the sky, the huge, shadowy Waianae Mountains.

The harbor was full of ships. Submarines, cruisers, destroyers.

There was a naval air station on Ford Island, where the big PBY patrol planes were based. Battleships were moored in pairs alongside Ford Island. Battleship Row. That's where he looked for his father's ship, the *Arizona*. He knew where it was moored, and there it was, the signal flags snapping in the wind.

He stood, straddling his bike, and saluted. He did it impulsively. It was corny, true, but he was really happy to see his father's ship. A lot of corny things were true. The military was corny, all the spit-and-polish stuff, but it was true, too. He had been on the *Arizona* on family days with his mother and sister, the officers and enlisted men in dress whites, standing at attention under the giant fourteen-inch guns, and the *Arizona* band playing.

Afterward, there were movies and ice cream on the fantail, and Adam's father taking him around, embarrassing him by introducing him to every officer as "a future navy man."

He watched a motor launch leave the *Arizona* and head across the bay toward the navy yards and the main docks. The boat, trailing a long frothy wake, was loaded with white-capped sailors headed for shore leave. His father might be among them, or he might be home already. Officers with families could live off ship when they were in port.

Adam started back to Honolulu, pedaling hard. It was exciting when his father came back from a cruise, but it was tense, too. His father liked them all there to welcome him: his crew lined up to greet their commander. If Adam was late, things could get off on the wrong foot. It would take him an hour to get home. He stood up on the pedals and pushed harder.

"Daddy's here," Bea screamed. They were all in the garden. His mother was wearing a silk dress, a pink flower in her hair. His father was stretched out on a lawn chair in his dress whites with the high collar and the single row of neat, shiny buttons. He'd taken off his shoes and socks.

"Dad," Adam said, and he saluted because he knew his father liked that.

"Your hair," his father said.

"Sorry, sir." Adam brushed his hair quickly to one side. In a second it was going to fall back the way it always did. His father's hair was blond and wavy and stayed put. Adam's was dark, and it flopped all over the place. He never thought about how it looked except around his father.

When his father was home, everything Adam did was with him in mind. It wasn't that his father demanded things or gave a lot of orders. It was just that he was there, and that changed everything.

"Ten days and look at him," his father said approvingly to Adam's mother. His father wasn't big, but he had a big presence and a big voice, too. "What have you been feeding him, Marilyn?"

"I hadn't noticed, but you're right. He is taller, isn't he?"

"Wiggle them, Daddy." Bea was leaning over their father's knees, examining his bare toes. "Say the five little sailors."

It was a story his father told. "The big boy toe is Rip," his father said, "then comes Lip." Bea touched each toe as he named it. "Then Chip, then Hip, and little bitty—"

"Bip," Bea said. "Now tell the girl toes."

"Five little tarts. Suzi's the biggest, then comes Doozi, then Choozi, then Bloozi, then—"

"Bea! Me!" she said loudly. "Then they get married. Say that part, Daddy. Say it fast."

"Rip to Suzi, Lip to Doozi, Chip to Choozi, Hip to Bloozi, and Bip to—"

"Me!" Bea yelled.

They all laughed. Adam's mother went into the kitchen to make a pitcher of lemonade.

"How's school?" his father asked.

"It's okay."

"Making friends?"

"Oh, sure."

"Civilian schools are different, aren't they?"

"It's not that bad," Adam said.

His father picked up Bea and marched around with her. "What if I walked around my ship this way, Bumble Bea, in my bare feet? What do you think my men would say?"

"No bare feet in the navy, Daddy. That's against the rules."

"Dad, can I have the keys to the car?" Adam said. His father was in such a good mood.

"What for?"

"To practice my driving."

"Since when do you take the car?"

"Just around the house," Adam said. There was never any traffic up here. His mother had let him practice a few times while his father was away.

"You don't drive alone till you get your license."

"I don't go anywhere," Adam said. "Honestly, Dad. Just up and down the street around the house. I stay real close."

"Don't even think of it," his father said, but a moment later—he was in a really good mood—he reversed himself. "Okay, get the car keys and let's see what you can do."

Adam got behind the wheel, and his father took the passenger seat. "Always put the car in neutral," his father said.

Adam nodded and turned the key. The needles moved on the gauges—the gas, the heat, the oil, and the ammeter, which showed the electric charge. He pulled out the choke.

"You don't need to do that."

"I thought—"

"We just drove in, so the engine is still hot."

He pushed the choke in. "Right." He knew it. Why hadn't he remembered that you only choked a cold engine?

He didn't drive well. He'd done a lot better other times. He either let the clutch out too fast or didn't feed enough gas. The car bucked. "Ride 'em, cowboy," his father said. He was still cheerful, but Adam was a mess. He stalled a couple of times, and then he backed into their neighbor's hibiscus hedge.

"Stop!" his father ordered. "Whoa! Hold it!"

Adam got the car back on the driveway. His father didn't say anything else, but Adam was done. He didn't want to practice anymore.

"Good," his father said, taking the keys. "You got the idea. A little more practice on the fine points, and you'll be okay."

"Thanks, Dad." Adam went to his room and flopped down on the bed. He felt exhausted.

4

"Hey, Snowman!"

Davi Mori, the kid with the sleepy eyes and the sticky brain, was calling Adam. They had a couple of classes together, and whenever Davi saw him, it was, "Hey, Snowman." Adam couldn't figure the kid out. Maybe he wanted to be friends, but all he talked about was snow. He was at it again.

"How cold is snow?" he asked. "If you hold snow in your hand, how long does it take to melt? How high does it pile up?"

Adam held his hand over his head as high as he could reach.

"Baloney, haole boy."

"Believe it or don't, I don't care. Would you believe ten feet of snow?"

"So how do you get out of your house?"

"Climb out the upstairs window."

"You are a straight-faced haole liar." Davi walked away.

Later that day, Adam saw Davi again. Well, he didn't see him till Davi smashed into him in the hall. "Out of my way, haole boy." And he was gone. Hit and run.

"Is that the Hawaiian way of being friendly?" Adam yelled after him.

Davi came right back and challenged him to a punching

contest. Adam was bigger than Davi and heavier. "Not a good idea," Adam said.

"Afraid to take a punch?" Davi said, and punched him, no warning, nothing. Punched him hard.

Adam rubbed his shoulder. "You are a real jerk." Not correct behavior. You were never supposed to let on that you'd been hurt, but he didn't care. He started to walk away, but Davi got in his way and offered his shoulder.

"Hit me," he said. "It's your turn. Hit me as hard as you can."

Adam's father always said what made a throw a throw and a punch a punch was follow-through. *Punch like you're going to put the other guy through the wall.*

Adam punched Davi, gave it all he had, a really solid punch.

It took Davi a moment to get his breath. Then he shrugged. "I've been hit harder by a marshmallow."

After that they had a kind of friendship, if you could call it that. Whenever they met, they exchanged insults and pounded each other.

Then, at a general assembly early in December, Adam got a big surprise. It was a Friday, the last day of school that week, and there was Davi up on the stage reading his winning essay in the American Legion "I'm Proud to Be an American" Contest. He stood in front of the whole school and read in a voice that carried to the last row of the auditorium, where Adam was sitting. A man from the American Legion who stood ramrod straight presented Davi with a ten-dollar check.

Adam tried to be unimpressed, but he had to admit that

standing up there was not something that he could see himself doing. And besides, Davi's essay really was good.

Later that afternoon, in biology lab, where they had teamed up to do the frog dissections, Adam congratulated Davi. Sort of. "That's some voice you've got," he said. "Have you thought about a career calling in pigs?"

Davi swung. Adam ducked, and they ended up horsing around till the teacher got fed up and put them at opposite ends of the room.

"Look," Bea said, holding up her stuffed animal. It was Saturday morning and she was sitting on Adam's bed. "Bear says good morning to Adam."

Bea was still in her nightgown. She slept in an alcove in a corner of their parents' room. Adam's room was off the kitchen. The model planes he'd built hung from the ceiling. They were never still.

Bea pushed her teddy bear in his face. "Bear says time to kiss." Adam put down the model plane he'd been maneuvering and gave Bear an extra-loud kiss. "Stop it." She pinched his nose. "Do you want to play?"

"Surely, little girl." He gave her his newest Japanese fighter plane. "It's called a Zero, and this game is called dogfight."

"I don't like dogs who fight."

"It's not dogs fighting, it's planes fighting each other the way they do it in a war. This is the way we play. You're high, against the sun, so I can't see you till the last second, and you come out of the sun, shooting down at me."

"You don't shoot your brother."

"It's only a game." He moved her arm so her plane was above his. "Make believe you're going to shoot me."

"I can do it," she said, pushing his hand away. "You don't have to show me. *Bap! Bap! Bap!*"

"Good! See how you're behind me, on my tail? It looks bad for me, but watch this." He sent his navy Corsair into a rolling dive and came back up under the Zero. "You see that? I just blew your plane into a thousand pieces."

"You did not." Bea held her plane up triumphantly. "See, you missed me."

"Okay, test time," he said. "What's the Punchbowl?"

"Where we live."

"Do you know it's a dead—"

"Volcano! I know that already."

"Do you know that Hawaii is built on all dead volcanoes that came out of the ocean?"

"You told me." She yawned, patting her mouth. "That is so boring."

He picked up another model plane with square-tipped wings. "What's this plane called?"

"I don't know. No fair."

"Grumman Wildcat. It's the navy fighter plane. And this one here, next to it, is a P-40 Curtiss Warhawk. It's the army fighter, and this one's a German Messerschmitt Me 109."

"Which plane is the best?"

"The American planes are always the best."

"We always win," Bea said.

"Hello . . ." Their mother looked in. "Anybody home? It's time for breakfast."

"We're playing dogfight," Bea said. "*Bap, bap, bap!* I won, Mommy."

"Is it really time for breakfast, Mom?" Adam asked.

"It's almost time for lunch, kiddo. Let's clear the decks and get this bunk ready for inspection."

When his father was home, their house was a ship. The floors were decks, beds were bunks, windows were portholes, the kitchen was the galley, and if Adam said "bathroom," his father said, "I think you mean the head."

"Your father sees this mess, you're in for a lecture," his mother said.

"And maybe a sock on the behind," Bea said. "And you're going to cry and cry."

"Let me remind you, little girl," Adam said, "boys don't cry."

He lifted her off his bunk, then made it navy style, by the book, everything taut, hospital corners, no wrinkles. His father was still asleep, so his mother would do the inspection. It was their regular Saturday-morning ritual, whether his father was here or not.

When he was ready, he called her, then stood by the door. His mother did a tough inspection. There was always some place he'd forgotten to dust. It was the shelf in the closet this time. When his father did the inspection, he'd bounce a quarter on the bunk and if it didn't bounce high enough for him to catch, Adam would have to tear the bunk apart and make it over again.

After his mother had finished the inspection and he had wiped the shelf, she interrogated him exactly as his father did, even deepening her voice. "Do you appreciate that you have a room of your own, sailor?"

"Yes, sir, I do!"

"I didn't have a room of my own when I was a boy, sailor."

"No, sir, I know that."

His mother stood at attention. She enjoyed this little game they played. "All I ever got for Christmas was a pair of itchy red socks. No model airplanes, no Raleigh racers."

"No, sir," he said. "I know that, sir!"

"Are you thankful for what you have?"

"Yes, sir, I am. I know that I'm one fortunate son of a gun. And I have to give back, I know that, too. Yes, sir, I am a grateful boy."

"Are you mocking me, sailor?"

"Yes, sir!"

"That's going to get you six months of KP, sailor."

In the kitchen a few minutes later, his mother put the yellow cornflakes box on the table with a bowl and a banana. Bea was on the floor playing with Bear. "I want Jell-O, please," she said. Koniko, their Japanese maid, didn't work on the weekends, although she'd be in later to baby-sit Bea. Adam and his parents were going to the movies.

Adam peeled the banana. "What was Dad like when he was my age, Mom?"

"He was a farm boy, and he had to work terribly, terribly hard. If there was work to be done, he got up at five every morning before school. A lot of times he never made it to school. He was the oldest, and your grandpa needed him on the farm. Grandpa couldn't do a lot with just one arm."

Adam's grandfather Pelko had lost an arm in the Austro-Hungarian army during World War I. That arm ended just below the elbow. He usually kept a sock over the stump. He could always make Adam jump by wriggling the bare stump in his face.

"Dad ran away from home, didn't he?"

Adam knew the answer, but this was the thing about his father that most fascinated him. His father, so disciplined, so regular, so sober, was once free enough—or wild enough—that he left his family and took to the road. Fourteen years old, Adam's age. He had thought about that a lot. That was really brave.

His mother emptied the contents of a Jell-O package into a bowl. "Your father ran away, but he wasn't a bad kid. He joined the navy—"

"—And lied about his age," Adam said.

"Your father doesn't lie! I don't like the way you said that, Adam."

"Sorry," he said.

She poured boiling water over the Jell-O. "It wasn't the same as real lying. He wanted the navy. He needed a home. Sometimes life forces you to do things. We don't know how hard his life was, Adam. We can't even imagine it. He had to work like a man from the time he was eight years old. You will never have to make the choices he did."

She stirred the Jell-O. "And what he's accomplished, the position of trust and authority that he's risen to, everything he's achieved—he did it all by himself. He came up from nothing. Your father—I have to say it—your father is an admirable man. Really, a great man."

"Maybe he'll be admirable of the fleet someday."

A flip remark. It just sprang out of his mouth. He really agreed with his mother, his father *was* admirable, but there was something about his being so admirable that, well, scared Adam. Would he ever be capable of doing what his father did? Could he ever be even half the man his father was?

If his mother caught the *admirable* pun, she didn't let on. "There might be a war," she said. She refilled the teakettle.

"War with Japan?" he asked.

"Yes." She sighed. "Nobody wants it, but—"

"Dad wants it."

"What do you mean 'Dad wants it'? What kind of thing is that to say, Adam?"

"I mean that's his job, Mom. That's what all the training exercises are about. Don't worry, we're ready for them."

"Ready is one thing, war is something else."

"You don't have to worry, Mom. There's nothing safer than a battleship. If war comes, Dad's going to be okay."

He made his hand into a gun. War was exciting. It was action. It was ships, planes, and guns. It was being faster and smarter than your enemy. It was defending your country.

"Dad says all that talk in Washington is a waste of time. The Japs want to push us out of the Pacific, but if they try, we're going to knock their heads off."

"Don't say 'Jap,'" his mother said. "It's vulgar."

"Sorry, Mom."

He put his bowl in the sink. He just hoped that if war came, it wouldn't be over too soon. "I'm going out now," he said.

"Get me some papayas first," his mother said.

He stepped out into the garden. The grass was wet and tickled his bare feet. It was December, and there were flowers in the bushes and bird sounds in the air, and everywhere there was the smell of summer. A big, ugly toad sat under the papaya tree. Adam inched his foot toward it. "Buffo," he said, and it jumped away.

He picked a few papayas and brought them in to his mother. "I'll be back at 1800."

"Where are you going?"

Where was he going? He didn't know. "I'm just going to poke around."

"Be home on time. You know your father."

"Don't worry, Mom, I'll be here."

Adam, on his bike, stood high up off the seat, riding the pedals. The palms and the monkeypod trees turned the street into a long green tunnel. Flowers flashed by—red and white and lavender—on every lawn and house. He was going nowhere in a hurry. Nobody to meet, no friend, no game waiting, but it was good to be moving.

He rode down Punchbowl Street, past the Iolani Palace, the home of the Hawaiian kings and queens, and the statue of Kamehameha the Great, a Hawaiian general who had united the islands more than one hundred years ago. He rode through the downtown area to the pier, then turned up along the shore.

A jumble of little cottages was plunked down near the ocean. Narrow lanes and cars parked every which way. Sand everywhere, the buildings weathered, faded and battered almost flat by the sun.

The sky was a cloudless blue. The wind gusted, and the ocean rose and fell. Frothy rollers rippled toward the shore. In the distance Adam saw sampans and Japanese fishing boats.

"Flarraaah . . ." A tiny Japanese woman was selling flowers door-to-door. "Flarraaah . . ." she sang.

He walked his bike down to the water. The beach was almost empty. Nearby was the Royal Hawaiian Hotel, and beyond it, the Moana and the Halekulani, where his parents went to dance.

Suddenly a bunch of boys burst from a lane and onto the beach. Some were on bikes, some were running. They were tossing a ball back and forth.

Adam wouldn't have minded playing, but they were all Hawaiian kids, and he didn't know them. Then someone yelled, "Haole!" It was Davi Mori, barefoot and wearing a pair of old pants and one of those flowered Hawaiian shirts. "Hey, haole! You wanna play?"

Adam hesitated. He was glad to see Davi, but he never knew what to think of that haole stuff.

"We need one more player," Davi said.

"What's the game?"

Davi tossed a coconut to him. "Football, only we play it with a coconut."

"Ah, so. Coconut ball," Adam said, and he was sorry. It sounded too much like a Charlie Chan movie. Maybe Davi would think he was making fun of him.

"Tackle is one knee down," Davi said.

"Okay."

"Come on, then."

The others were waiting. "This is my friend Adam," Davi said. "He's on my team."

The other team leader was a big, noisy kid called Martin Kahahawai. "What you need the haole for, Mori? No brains of your own?"

"You got five on your team. Now I got five."

The end zones were marked in the sand. Sidelines, too.

"We're the Devil Sharks," Davi said.

"Hey," Martin said, "that's Hawaiian."

"So?"

"You're a Jap."

"And you're a moron. You can have Devil Sharks." Davi turned to the others. "Give us a name, quick."

"Uhrr . . ."

"Mmmmm . . ."

"Ahhh . . ."

"Barracudas," a dark, skinny kid named Joseph said.

"Rattlesnakes."

"How about Sea Scouts?"

"Too much like Boy Scouts."

"How about Girl Scouts?"

"Sure, we can be the Girl Scout Cookies."

"Wildcats," Adam said.

"Wildcats?" Davi said.

"Like the F4F navy fighter."

"Nah," Davi said, but then Martin said, "Devil Sharks eat Wildcats for breakfast."

That did it. "Let's go, Wildcats," Davi said.

Davi's team got the coconut first. The guys were talking back and forth, watching each other but never saying anything to Adam, not even looking at him. Davi was the quarterback. He faked a throw to the left, then ran to the right and got past the whole Shark team, all the way to the end zone.

"Hey, Sharks," Davi said, "that was so easy."

Now the Devil Sharks had the coconut. "Martin's going to keep it," Davi said. "So pile up on him."

"What if he passes?" Adam asked.

"You'll see, he won't."

Martin ran like a truck in low gear, but those arms and legs of his knocked the Wildcats off left and right. Nobody could bring him down. He went through them like a bowling ball through a bunch of tenpins.

"I told you guys," Davi kept saying. "You got to hang on to him."

Adam had his hands up for the ball a lot, but Davi never threw to him. He kept passing to the other guys, especially Joseph, who made two touchdowns. But then the next time Joseph carried the ball, Martin popped it out of his hands and ran with it. It looked like another sure Martin touchdown.

"Stop him," Davi shouted. "Get him!"

Adam caught up to Martin. Then he was in front of Martin, trying to slow him down, until Martin tripped and they both fell. "Got him, you got him!" Davi shouted. After that Adam felt more like part of the team.

They took their shirts off and played away the afternoon.

Afterward, they threw themselves into the ocean, then sat around near the ashes of a fire and insulted one another.

"Hey, Slant Eye . . ."

"What, Moonface?"

"You look like a cat with diarrhea."

"You look like a rat with a bellyache."

"You call that an insult?"

Adam didn't say much, just sat next to Davi and listened.

One of the boys cracked open the coconut with a rock. They all took pieces. "First time I ever ate fresh coconut," Adam said.

"Haole boy," Martin said. "You're getting to be a real Hawaiian. You know Kamapua'a?"

"Who?" Adam asked.

"Kamapua'a, the great Hawaiian pig god."

"Pig god—you're kidding me, right?"

Martin eyed him contemptuously. "The great pig god, Kamapua'a, he got eight eyes, eight legs, forty toes. He eat the valleys, swallow volcanoes whole. He brushes his teeth with trees. When he farts, he make all the islands shake. What do you say, haole boy? You got a god like that?"

Adam half smiled. Was Martin pulling his leg?

"You sure he a haole?" Martin asked Davi. "He don't act that smart to me."

"You got a fish brain," Davi said.

"And you got a mush brain."

They were still at the insults when Adam thought to look at the time. It was 1700, and he was supposed to be home in an hour. His father would be waiting. "See you!" he said, and ran for his bike.

Davi came with him and they rode along together, talking about food they didn't like and songs they did. "I really like 'On the Road to Mandalay,'" Adam said.

". . . where the flying fishes play," Davi sang.

They were singing at the top of their voices. Adam never

saw the hole in the road. He was thrown from the bike—gravel in his palms. That was okay. What wasn't okay was his bike. The steering wheel was all wobbly. Something was cracked and it was impossible to ride. "What am I going to do now? I can't go home with the bike this way."

"My dad'll fix it," Davi said.

"Your dad?"

"Yeah. He can fix anything."

Adam hesitated. If he went with Davi he'd be late, but if he had to walk all the way home, he'd be late too. And with a broken bicycle.

Davi lived downtown near Hotel Street, where sailors went on leave, where Adam's parents had told him never to go. The area was called Chinatown, but Davi said mostly Japanese people lived here now. He led the way down one narrow alleyway and then another, some of them so crowded that the balconies almost touched. He stopped in front of a yard halfcovered with weeds. His father was in back, working on a flatbed truck. A skinny man with bony arms and big teeth.

Adam knew he shouldn't even think it, but Davi's father looked like one of those crazy Japs in a comic book.

"This is my friend, Adam," Davi said.

His father sat down on the edge of the truck, wiping his hands on a rag and talking to Davi in Japanese.

"Talk English, Dad," Davi said, glancing at Adam.

"Very happy to make your acquaintance." Mr. Mori hopped down and bowed from the waist, his hands at his side.

To make up for his mean thought, Adam bowed back.

"Hey!" Davi punched him. "Quit kidding around. You don't have to do that stuff."

His father examined the bike, muttering under his breath. Adam was pretty sure he was saying something like "stupid kid" in Japanese.

Davi brought over a welding cart holding two gas tanks. He unwound cables, turned gauges, and handed his father the brass welding torch and a pair of dark goggles. Mr. Mori lit the torch and adjusted the hissing flame from yellow to blue. He pulled down the goggles, and with a long metal rod he welded Adam's bike. He did it in a minute.

When the weld had cooled, he wire-brushed it clean, then bounced the bike up and down a couple of times. "Good!" he said. "Fixed good."

Adam rode the bike around the yard. It was solid again. "Thanks!" he said. "Thanks a lot! How much?" He put his hand in his pocket. Davi's father shook his head and went back to work on the truck.

"I can pay," Adam said.

"Forget it," Davi said. "He did it because you're my friend."

The torch had burned away paint along the side of the repair. Davi dipped a brush in a can of red paint and painted over the weld.

"Thanks," Adam said again. "I better get going now."

"What's the rush?"

"My dad will kill me if I'm late."

"He'll understand. You had an accident. You couldn't help that. Besides, the paint has to dry. You want to see my room?"

Adam let himself be persuaded, and followed Davi through a gate in a high hedge into a shaded garden with several low buildings. A long, low table with an oilcloth tacked on top sat under a lattice of vines and red flowers, and a wooden icebox leaned against one of the sheds.

Adam followed Davi into the biggest shed. It smelled like seaweed and vinegar. "Mama?" Davi called. On the wall, in a niche, gleaming out of the dimness, was a portrait of a mustached man sitting stiffly on a white horse.

"That's Hirohito," Adam said, showing off a little. "Your honorable emperor."

"Not mine," Davi said emphatically. "My parents think he's divine, like a living god, but they were born over there. In Japan. But I was born here. One hundred percent American. They're issei, and I'm nisei. That's what we say. Come on."

They went out and into another shed. It was Davi's.

The room was open up to the rafters, where a paper lantern and an orange paper fish hung. A table in front of the window held rocks and shells and pieces of coral. On one wall, Davi had tacked pictures of birds he'd cut from magazines. "I like anything with wings," he said.

"Airplanes, too?"

"No. Living things."

Above his cot Davi had tacked a calendar with a picture of the steamship *Lurline* with its high white hull and two big, fat stacks.

"We came on that ship," Adam said, "from the mainland. Four days. I puked my guts out."

"I never puke," Davi said. "I go on my uncle's fishing boat all the time."

Adam checked out Davi's books. *The Call of the Wild* by Jack London, and four Tarzan books by Edgar Rice Burroughs. "Yeah, I've read these," he said. He was ready to go—he had to go—but then they started talking again, about fishing this time. By the time Adam left, they had agreed to go fishing the next morning.

"Meet you no later than six," Davi said as they walked out.

"0600? You going to be up?" Adam said.

"I always get up that early. I like the light. You ever look at early-morning light?"

Adam shrugged. "I never thought about it."

"Look at it tomorrow morning."

Funny guy, Adam thought. He had a foot up on the bike pedal. "I'll take a long look and tell you what I think. I've got to go. My father—"

"Why do you worry about your father so much? What's he going to do if you're late, eat you?"

"Yeah. With ketchup. In small bites."

7

Adam went around the side of the house to stow his bike in the shed. He was late. He got a glass of milk in the kitchen and went out to face his father. His parents were sitting in the garden with their neighbor, Mrs. Parker, having afternoon cocktails. His parents were both dressed to go out, his father in his high-necked dress whites, and his mother in a white dress and high heels. Bea was playing in the grass near them.

"I know I'm late—" Adam began.

"Ah, there he is," Mrs. Parker said, raising her cigarette. "The little hero, the tall drink of water." She always had something funny to say, but he liked her.

"Milk," he said, holding up his glass. "Tall drink of milk."

Mrs. Parker smiled and stood up. "See you folks later." She went through the hedge to her house.

Adam's father leaned back, hands behind his head. "You were going to be home early, Adam—1800, I believe, and it's now . . ." He looked at his watch.

"Sorry, Dad." He explained about the bike and the hole in the road, and how he didn't see it till too late. "It was that god—" He almost swore, but his father stopped him.

"Watch your mouth. You don't talk that way in front of your mother."

"Sorry. Sorry." He couldn't stop saying "sorry." "My bike was broken, Dad. Davi's father welded it back together."

"Who's Davi?"

"He's a friend of mine from school. His father wouldn't take any money, and the bike is as good as new now."

"Who are these people? Where do they live?"

"Chinatown."

"Chinese?"

"No." Something in his father's voice put Adam off saying anything about his plans for the morning. "They're Japanese."

"Tomorrow you bring Mr. Tojo, or whatever his name is, a dollar for his work. And I expect there are plenty of other boys for you to make friends with."

"Davi's the smartest boy in our class, Dad."

"That may well be, but I want you to think about things. Like who he is and who you are." His father picked up his cocktail, took a sip, then handed the glass to his mother. "Can you get me some more ice, Marilyn?"

"I'll get it, Dad," Adam said.

"No, I want to talk to you." His mother went back in the house. "Sit down, son," his father said.

Adam sat at the edge of the seat. He knew what was coming.

"Adam, I am an officer in the navy. This is a military family." He was keeping time with his foot, giving Adam the drill, marching him through it. "I shouldn't have to be telling you this. You know this. What you do reflects on your family. Reflects on me and reflects on the United States Navy."

"I know, Dad."

"The navy has been good to me. I grew up in the navy. I became a man in the navy. It's given me everything. And what it's given me, it's given you, too. You know that the searchlight is always on me. On me, on us, on our family. Our conduct has to be above reproach. Do you understand? You wouldn't want me to do anything that would bring shame on me or the navy."

"You never would," Adam said.

"Correct, because I think about what I do, who I associate with, who my friends are. And that's what I want you to do. Think!" His father leaned forward and tapped Adam on the knee. "We're very close to war with Japan. That's why we're here in Honolulu, in Pearl. Listen, Adam, I have nothing against this boy you've met. There are a lot of them here. Forty percent of the Hawaiian Territory is Japanese. This is the most Japanese city in the world outside of Japan. There are some navy people who think they're all spies. I'm not that way myself, but I would not be friends, at this time, with any-one who is Japanese."

"Davi's an American," Adam said. "Nisei. That's what that means. He was born in this country. Dad, he won the American Legion contest!"

"Your friend may have been born here, but his parents weren't. Am I right?"

Adam nodded.

"They are Japanese first. Just as you are an American first. Their allegiance is to their country, just as ours is to our country. And when the war starts, what are they going to do?

Nobody knows exactly, but count on it, they're going to be a big problem here in Hawaii."

His mother had returned with their drinks. "Emory," she said, "maybe the war situation isn't as bad as we think. I was just listening to the radio, and our secretary of state is talking to the Japanese ambassador in Washington at this very minute."

"All I'm saying is we have to be careful. I want Adam to be careful. We just don't know. I can't have anyone saying that Lieutenant Emory Pelko's son has a friend who's a—"

"What about Koniko?" Adam interrupted. "And Hideko? They're both here every day, right in our house. Everyone we know has Japanese working for them."

"I'm not concerned about that. They work, we pay them. This town, all of Hawaii, the sugar plantations and the pineapple industry, they'd all close down without them. I'm just telling you, a friend is something else. It doesn't matter what you think or I think, we're judged by our friends. And whatever you do comes back on me."

Adam was silent. His father was saying he had to give up Davi.

"Adam," his father said. "It's not like there's a shortage of boys."

Adam nodded and stood up.

"Am I talking to myself?"

"I heard you, sir." His jaw was tight. Everything in him was tight. He couldn't talk, couldn't look at his father, he didn't want to.

Just then Bea created a commotion. She came running out of the house, followed by Koniko. "I want to go to the movies with you," Bea cried.

"Too late for baby," Koniko said, trying to catch Bea, but she couldn't run fast enough in her kimono.

"Koniko's right," Adam's mother said. "It's too late for you to stay up, honey. You're not old enough for the movies."

"I can stay up! I am old enough. I'm not going to sleep. I don't want to stay alone with Koniko."

"Oh, look at Koniko," his mother said. "Look how sad she is. You're hurting her feelings."

Koniko tried to pick up Bea, but Bea squirmed out of her arms. "Adam!" she cried.

He picked her up and whispered in her ear, "I'll bring you a Mary Jane if you're a good girl."

"A whole Mary Jane?" She put her arms around his neck. "All for me?"

"I won't even ask you for a bite, but you have to stop crying and stay with Koniko."

By the time he got her settled and they'd picked out a story-book to read, his father was calling. "Rats," Adam said.

"You said a bad word. I know a bad word too."

"You do?"

"I have to whisper," she said. "*Shutup*."

Adam rolled his eyes. "Really bad," he said.

After his father parked the car, they strolled over to Palm Boulevard. The air was sweet. Not even the car fumes could change that. It was Saturday night, and the city was dark, blurry, and soft. Even the cars purred.

Walking behind his parents, Adam was conscious of the click of his mother's high heels and the regular measure of his father's step. He matched his step to his father's, a steady beat, as if the two of them were one step, one heart. *I'm not fighting you, Dad. I understand about the navy and our family and all that, but it doesn't seem fair. It's not even Davi so much—it's being told who I can be friends with.*

Sailors who passed on the sidewalk saluted his father. Adam saw some boys from school and sort of saluted them, half raised his hand. "Yeah," they said. "Hi, Adam."

The movie theater was full of white uniforms. Adam stopped at the candy counter to buy the Mary Jane for Bea, then joined his parents. He sat down next to his mother, sank down, and propped his knees against the seat in front of him. His father reached over and tapped him, and he sat up and put both feet squarely on the floor.

The theater darkened, and a picture of the flag came on the screen. They all stood and saluted while "The Star-Spangled Banner" was played. Then they sat down again, and the cartoon came on, Bugs Bunny, then the *March of Time* newsreel, then the movie, *The Great Dictator.* The last Charlie Chaplin movie that Adam had seen was *Modern Times.* He'd liked that a lot, especially when Charlie got caught in the gears in the factory. This one made fun of Hitler and Mussolini, and it was pretty funny, but not as good as he'd expected.

What he really remembered afterward was the newsreel and

the war pictures, and the commentator's deep, authoritative voice. "The German army is on the attack in Russia!" Pictures of German paratroopers sliding down the wing of a cargo plane, like penguins sliding off a shelf of ice. Next a picture of an Italian ship sinking off North Africa, the sailors leaping into the ocean. "Look at that, ladies and gentlemen. You are watching a war from a ringside seat!" The last segment was a training film of American soldiers bayoneting canvas bags that were supposed to be enemy soldiers. "Look at our boys!" the commentator said. "Look at them go! Fool with America, and you stir up a hornet's nest, and we know how to sting!"

Adam clapped and cheered with everyone else, but when he glanced over at his mother, her eyes were shut tight. She couldn't bear violence, even fake bayoneting of a canvas bag. His father was looking at her too. He winked at Adam.

Okay! Adam took a deep breath. His father wasn't mad at him anymore.

When they got home, Koniko gave Adam's father a message to call the base. The duty officer had a family emergency, and Adam's father was needed to cover for him. "I should be home sometime tomorrow," he said, kissing Adam's mother. He was going to drop Koniko off at her home on his way to the base. "Maybe in the afternoon. Bye, son."

"Bye, Dad," Adam called over his shoulder. He was on his way to put the Mary Jane on Bea's pillow.

In the morning Adam ate a doughnut and left his mother a note: BE BACK SOON. He drew a little stick figure for Bea, showing himself on his bike.

He carried the bike out to the street. It was early. Sleeping houses. Shiny lawns. Their paper hadn't been delivered yet. Not a car in sight. Nobody around but him.

All the way to the cannery, Adam kept thinking that if Davi didn't show up, it would be a relief. He wouldn't have to say anything or make excuses for not wanting to go fishing. He'd see Davi in school, and they could be friends there.

Davi had said six o'clock, under the giant pineapple. Adam checked his watch: 0600. He was here, but Davi wasn't. Adam decided to wait fifteen minutes, tops, and then to go home.

"Hey, haole!" It was Martin, the big Hawaiian kid, pedaling a bike with Davi sitting on the crossbar holding the fishing poles.

"Adam!" Davi held up the poles. "I've got one for you too."

Now was the moment to tell Davi *I'm not going fishing. Can't. Sorry. Something's come up.* . . . Simple. But saying it to Davi's face was a lot different than thinking it. "You're late," he said.

Davi gestured at Martin. "I had to wake him up. He sleeps like a pig."

"Like a pig god," Adam said, to say something.

Martin belched. He took the poles and lashed them to the crossbar on Adam's bike.

Say it, Adam told himself. But the poles were tied to the bike, and all the things he'd thought to say sounded like lies and excuses, which they were. It would be stupid to say anything now. Davi wouldn't understand. And Martin—Adam didn't even want to think what Martin would say.

They rode out on Kamehameha Highway, going west, toward Pearl Harbor. Adam watched Martin's broad back, the bike going from one side to the other, as if he owned the road. "We're fishing in Pearl?" Adam said. Davi looked back and nodded. They were pedaling all over the road. It dipped and rose. There was almost no traffic. Only once, going up a rise, a taxi loaded with sailors came shooting down at them, and they had to scramble to get out of the way.

"Close call," Davi said.

"They almost got us that time," Adam said.

"Short fishing trip," Martin said. They were all laughing. "Haole boy," Martin said, "you going catch a big fish?"

"Hope so," Adam said. He rode alongside Martin.

"You ever eat Hawaiian fish? The best. You eat mahi mahi, you know you ate fish, man. You wrap that fish in taro leaf, then put it in hot coals." Martin licked his lips.

"You ever eat brook trout?" Adam said. "You catch them in ice-cold water, then you fry them over an open fire." His father and he had done that in the mountains in Tennessee last summer.

"Best fish come from the ocean," Martin said, and he reeled

off the names of fish Adam had never heard of. "*Aholehole*, big-eye *akule, uhu, ahi*. Use *ahi* head to catch crab. You watch me," he said. "Fish jump out of the water for Hawaiians." He arced his hand into the air. "*Whiiish! Whiiish!* We just put out our hands and they jump in. Ask Davi!"

"It's true, man," Davi said.

They were almost all the way to Aiea when they stopped near a grove of eucalyptus trees. They followed a track along the edge of a field, then walked their bikes down the hill toward the harbor. Spread out before them were the white oil-storage tanks and the red-roofed buildings of the naval station, the destroyers and cruisers bunched together, and the dark bulk of Ford Island.

They stashed the bikes in a bamboo thicket and walked along a wire fence. Just beyond a sign saying MILITARY PERSONNEL ONLY Davi slid under the fence where the ground was worn smooth, and Martin went after him. It crossed Adam's mind that they could get caught. *What you do reflects on your family*. But he just couldn't make himself believe that his going fishing could ruin his father's career. Anyway, his father was never going to know.

"You coming, haole boy?" Martin said, and Adam slid under. It was as easy as that.

They scrambled down to the water's edge, sending stones tumbling. Shorebirds flew up, and ripples fanned out across the water. Pearl Harbor was like glass, calm and quiet. Shadows lay along the shore. The sun was still below the mountains.

Martin went poking along the shore, while Davi and Adam stood on a rock, looking out across the water. Everything seemed closer down here—the wharves and docks, the dry docks, where ships were repaired, the cranes and hooks and overhead slings. The battleships moored along Ford Island seemed close enough to touch.

"It's like a pearl," Davi said.

"What—the harbor?"

"The light."

Adam nodded, and they just stood there for a while, looking at everything.

"What you doing?" Martin called. "Come here." He had a cigarette in hand, and he was squatting over a little pile of rocks. "We ask stonefish god to help us out. Ku'ula," he said, "bring us lotta fish." He blew smoke over the rocks. "Okay. Now the fish are going come to us."

Davi took the cigarette from Martin, puffed a couple of times, and blew smoke over the stonefish god. He handed the cigarette to Adam, who did the same.

"My dad give that to me," Martin said. "He said, 'Here, son, have a good smoke.'"

"Some story," Davi said.

Martin was looking at the battleships lined up along Ford Island. "Look at those big buggas. Which one's your father's?"

Adam pointed. "The one closest to us is the *Nevada* and just fore of that is the *Arizona*. That's my father's ship."

"Look at all those guns. How many?"

"Twelve fourteen-inch guns."

Martin whistled.

"Those big battleships, they're bigger than two football

fields put together. Each one has a displacement of more than thirty thousand pounds. They carry a thousand sailors."

Adam couldn't stop. He loved those ships. They were so powerful and so graceful, floating fortresses, the most powerful warships in the world. "They've got fourteen-inch armor plate. Bullets bounce off them, even bombs can't get through. They have so much firepower, nothing and nobody can touch them. Those big guns you see, those long rifles, they can shoot a fifteen-hundred-pound shell twenty miles and hit the target."

"Like that." Martin flipped the cigarette as far as he could into the water.

They spread out along the shore, turning over rocks and wading in the water, looking for bait: worms, crayfish, little minnows, anything to dangle on the end of a line. Martin cupped his hands in the water, then stood up. He'd caught three minnows, which they put in a can. "You see, haole, Ku'ula provides."

"Martin, Adam," Davi called. "Look at this." He was down along the shore and had found a rowboat half hidden in some bushes. The oars were neatly placed together under the seat. "It must have drifted here," he said.

"What a find," Adam said. They had planned to fish from shore but the boat was too good to resist.

"Ku'ula provides," Martin said again.

They stowed the poles under the seat. Davi placed each oar into its oarlock. Adam sat down next to him, and Martin pushed them off.

Davi and Adam rowed together. The sun came up, and a breeze rippled across the harbor. Martin dropped his line in the water. He complained that they were rowing so fast, he couldn't keep his line down.

They stopped rowing, and for a moment they just sat there. The battleships were plainly in sight. Adam focused on the *Arizona*, his father's ship. Signal flags fluttered. It was almost time for reveille.

The rowboat bobbed in the water. All at once bugle calls sounded from every direction, and the bands on the ships started playing "The Star-Spangled Banner." Adam thought about his father on the fantail, standing at attention, saluting the flag, and then looking out in their direction, seeing the rowboat and the boys in it . . . and recognizing him.

He hunched over. "You know, Davi, we better move."

Just then he became aware of the whine of planes in the air. He looked up. High overhead, dozens of planes flew in formation, approaching from every direction. Some planes were coming in low over the water. *It must be some kind of military exercise*, Adam thought. *A war game.*

A plane flew across the water, straight at them. It roared over, so low Adam could see the silver belly and the wheels hanging down. So low the prop wash shook the boat.

"What the hell?" Davi said.

The plane was past them, climbing sharply.

"Navy cowboy," Martin said.

"Uh uh. It wasn't navy," Adam said. The markings were all wrong. Instead of bars and stripes he'd seen red circles, like on a Japanese plane. He wasn't sure, but he thought he'd seen something drop into the water. It looked like the pictures he'd seen of torpedoes.

"Maybe they're making a movie," Adam said. And then, as if he'd ordered it, there was an explosion and a thick cloud of smoke erupted over Ford Island.

"Sound effects," Martin said.

A moment later a blast of hot air battered them. There was another explosion. And another. "That sounds so real," Adam said. He had to shout to make himself heard over the noise.

"Maybe somebody made a mistake," Davi said.

"Big jerk," Martin said.

"Big trouble," Adam said.

They were all standing in the boat, laughing. Martin pointed at the planes, "shooting" at them with his finger.

Planes, bombs, explosions. It was almost real, Adam thought, the way a newsreel is real. You knew it was a movie you were watching, not the actual war, but while you were sitting there, watching, it felt real. All that was missing now was the announcer with the god-like big voice. *Those are enemy planes, ladies and gentlemen, and you are sitting in the front row. A ringside seat.*

Bombs came tumbling out of the planes like black sticks. Flames and smoke rose from the battleships. Flags were on fire.

"It's real," Adam said, half to himself. Those planes, shooting across the water, the wheels hanging down, the open cockpits, the red circles. All those red circles. Were the planes Vals? Japanese torpedo bombers? Or were they American planes marked like Japanese planes?

"Look at them!" Davi was standing on the seat, waving his arms, cheering as if he were at a ball game.

"Those are Japanese," Adam said. He didn't even know if it was true or if he was in some crazy weird dream. He couldn't stop thinking that it was just like the movies. But there was something very wrong with the thought because this wasn't the movies. It wasn't a dream. It wasn't make-believe. Those were real Japanese bombers, dropping real bombs.

Why was Davi cheering? What was he doing? Signaling them? Yes, signaling them! He was Japanese. Japanese first! Who had said to come to Pearl Harbor to "fish"? Who had "found" the boat? Who had gotten them out here? "Dirty Jap!" Adam dragged Davi down. He wanted to get him. Kill him. Drown him.

Martin grabbed Adam. "You crazy!" They were all tangled together, rolling around in the bottom of the boat. Martin forced Adam back on the seat. "Stupid," he said. "Crazy man! We got to get out of here."

Davi squatted in the stern, panting, rubbing his arms and staring at Adam. Martin thrust an oar in Adam's hand and took the other oar. "Row, or I'll bust your face."

They rowed hard, away from the battleships and the bombs. Water sprayed over them. The rowboat pitched one way and then the other. Then, before his eyes, the *Arizona* lifted up out of the water. That enormous battleship bounced up in the air like a rubber ball and split apart. Fire burst out of the ship. A geyser of water shot into the air and came crashing down. Adam was almost thrown out of the rowboat. He clung to the seat as it swung around. He saw blue skies and the glittering city. The boat swung back again, and he saw black clouds, and the *Arizona*, his father's ship, sinking beneath the water.

10

Everything happened at once. The plane . . . bullets darting across the water . . . screams . . . the boat shooting up into the sky.

Adam hung in the air. He saw the red circle on the fuselage, he saw the gunner in his black helmet, and below him he saw the empty rowboat. Then he was in the water, down under the water. Water in his nose and in his throat. He came up next to the boat—it was almost on top of him. He clung to the side, choking and spitting.

The boat rode up and down with the waves, and he hung there, staring at the ragged row of holes along one side. They were so regular they could have been made by a sewing machine needle.

Something awful had happened. The sky was black where the *Arizona* had been. "My god, my god, oh, my god." He clung to the side of the boat thinking, *It's Sunday morning, and we were fishing*.

Suddenly there was silence. He could hear the wind. The planes had cleared from the sky. *Our side is coming*, he thought, and he pulled himself half out of the water and looked around for Martin and Davi. He was afraid. He wanted to see them, and when he didn't, he didn't let himself think what he was thinking—that they were dead.

"Davi," he called. "Martin! Davi!" His stomach clenched. "Martin . . . Davi . . ."

He got in the boat. His back was burning, and when he touched it, there was blood on his hand. Had he been shot? He didn't know. Maybe a bullet had grazed him.

"Davi!" he shouted. "Martin!" He stood up. In the distance he saw something bobbing up and down in the water, maybe a piece of driftwood. Then an arm came out of the water and he saw Davi and, beside him, Martin.

11

There was only one oar in the boat. Adam used it like a canoe paddle, swinging it from one side to the other. "I'm coming," he yelled, but it was slow going. The boat kept swinging the wrong way, fighting him, bucking him like a mule.

He cursed and yelled. It was so hard to keep the boat on course. It was taking so long to get to Martin and Davi. He kept looking up, afraid the planes would come back. The sky was obscured by black smoke, but at moments it cleared and he saw the green sugarcane fields in the distance and beyond them the quiet mountains. It was unreal. It was all unreal: the battleships half sunk, the bullet holes in the boat, Davi and Martin in the water.

When he reached them—they were clinging to the other oar—he saw that something was wrong with Martin. Davi got right in the boat, but Martin wouldn't. He wouldn't. He wouldn't do anything. He was afraid to move. A splinter the size of a pencil was sticking out of his chest. It moved every time he breathed. It made Adam sick to look at it. "Take it out," he said.

"I can't. It's sticking out my back."

"No, it isn't," Davi said. "I told you it wasn't. I looked."

"I can't," Martin said. "Leave me alone."

Adam exchanged a glance with Davi. "You row," Davi said, "I'll hold him." He leaned over and grabbed Martin's shirt.

It was hard rowing with Martin like a dead weight in the water. Adam rowed, staring blindly at the battleships in front of him, like a city on fire.

At the opposite shore Adam slid the boat in among the pilings, then just sat there. He was exhausted.

It took him and Davi both to get Martin up the ladder to the pier. Martin was pale, as if all the blood had drained out of him. Davi went up first, reaching down to hold Martin. Adam supported him from behind. That was the way they went up, one rung at a time. When they reached the pier, Martin sank down beside a pile of gravel. He didn't say anything, but his eyes scared Adam. He patted Martin's shoulder. He didn't know what to say.

The pier was a twisted, chaotic mess. It was like an anthill that had been kicked open. Sheds and ships were torn apart. Men were running every which way, dragging water hoses, crouched behind gun emplacements. A black sedan was weaving its way down the pier, detouring around holes and hunks of concrete and torn metal and dangling wires.

"See that car?" Adam said to Davi. "Maybe they'll take Martin to a doctor."

Davi grunted. He was barely speaking to Adam. Adam wanted to tell Davi that he was sorry he'd grabbed him in the boat. He couldn't explain it. It was just something that happened, something stupid like hitting himself in the head with a brick. It was as if an evil spirit had grabbed him, taken him over. It had to do with his father and the *Arizona* and being scared to death.

He was going to apologize to Davi, but not now. The important thing now was to get help for Martin. Davi was talking to a sailor who was standing nearby with a pistol in his hand. Suddenly he hit Davi with the gun and knocked him down. "Jap!" he yelled. "I've got a Jap!"

Adam ran, yelling at the sailor, "Stop, don't! Stop it." He hardly knew what he yelled. "We're Americans, Americans."

Men came running and pulled the sailor away. Adam helped Davi up. He was shaking, and there was blood on his face. The black car had stopped near them. "Put him in," the driver said. "I'm taking wounded." She was wearing a Red Cross uniform.

Davi got into the car and Adam ran back for Martin. When the car was full, Adam jumped on the running board and hooked his arm around the center post. He put his head in the car. Martin and Davi were squeezed together in the backseat next to a couple of wounded men. "Here we go," Adam said, as the car started to move. "It's going to be okay." He wanted to reassure them and himself, too, that their luck was changing—his father was going to be okay, too. But the sight of the wounded men and Martin gasping for breath and Davi with his bruised face made him shut up.

The car turned when an explosion shook the pier and spun out of control. It swung one way and then the other. Adam was thrown off. The car was heading straight into the harbor, but at the last minute it righted itself and kept going.

12

For the first time Adam was alone, and fear came. He'd been going and going—one thing and then another and then another. No time to think, no time to be scared. Now Davi's bloodied face was in front of him . . . and Martin holding his chest . . . and himself in the water . . . and the *Arizona*, crumpled like a piece of paper.

He was tired. He was beyond tired. He was exhausted. He wanted to go home, to be in his own bed with a blanket over his head and not have to think or remember. It was all too strange, too awful.

He climbed down the ladder, back to the rowboat, thinking he'd row back to where they'd left the bikes and go home. But when he got in the rowboat, he couldn't do anything.

He sat, head down, arms wrapped around his knees. Water slapped against the pilings. The boat rocked, and Adam rocked with it. Maybe he slept. A chill wind woke him. He smelled smoke and heard muffled explosions.

He opened and closed his hands. He blinked his eyes and turned his neck. Everything worked. Reaching around, he touched the edge of the wound. It was raw and it stung. He couldn't believe he'd been shot. Soldiers were shot. Not kids. He looked down and counted his bare toes. *Suzi, Doozi . . .*

A small brown bird flitting among the pilings caught his

attention. It was carrying bits of straw to a hole in one of the timbers. Maybe the bird had a nest there. Davi would know. He'd ask him when he got back.

"Sailor!"

Up on the pier a man, one arm in a sling, was calling to Adam. With the light behind him, he looked huge. "Sailor," he called, "does that pile of crap hold water?"

"Yes, sir."

The man came down the ladder one-armed, but fast, and dropped into the boat. There were officer's bars on his collar. "Row," he ordered.

"Sir—" Adam began to explain that he was just a kid, not a sailor.

"Sailor, shut your mouth. Get this slop bucket moving."

Adam rowed out into the open. He didn't want to do it, didn't want to leave the safety of the pier. But it was just one more crazy thing in a crazy day. In the real world he knew what to expect. Sure, unexpected things happened, but most things happened in a regular way. Every day he got up, got dressed, and went to school. On Saturday he cleaned his room, and on Sunday they went to church. Not like this, where everything that happened was like nothing that had ever happened before.

"Row, sailor! Put your back into it." The officer swore. He swore at the Japanese, at their bad manners and their lousy timing. "Sunday morning, they sneak attack us? For God's sake, I was in bed with my wife. Row, sailor!"

"Where are we going, sir?"

"The *Westy*." He checked his watch.

"What time is it, sir?"

"Will you row and shut up!" He adjusted his arm in the sling. "It's 0850."

Adam fixed his eyes on the officer's big, chunky face. "Sir . . . Lieutenant Pelko, sir, do you know him?" Officers knew one another.

"Pelko? What kind of name is that? What ship?"

"The *Arizona*."

"The *Arizona*? Take a look," he said furiously. He pointed to where the smoke was thickest. "There, that! That! That's what's left of it, that pile of scrap. The USS *Arizona* is gone," he said bitterly.

Adam thought about his father, how clever he was, how he could do anything. He'd been in the navy a long time and he was so smart. He could have seen it coming and gotten out. Somehow he'd gotten off in time, before the ship was hit. Maybe he was on the *West Virginia* right now.

"Starboard, sailor, more starboard." The officer pushed down on the oar. His hand over Adam's was like a piece of carpet, warm and hairy. "Where do we get sailors like you? Babies!"

A launch passed close enough for the officer to jump to his feet and order it alongside. "Come on, move! Never mind tying on. Give me a hand!" Not waiting for anyone, he leaped across and fell into the launch, still shouting orders. A sailor on the launch grabbed for Adam and swung him aboard. The launch never stopped moving. The rowboat was left to drift.

As they passed the battleships—one after another—the men on the launch became silent. It was like an earthquake had hit. The

USS *Oklahoma* had turned over and was lying on its side, propellers sticking up in the air. The water around the once-proud battleship was thick with oil, and it stunk. Smoke and filth. Life rafts, pieces of boats, and men floundered in the watery debris.

The *West Virginia* was just aft of the *Arizona* and it was on fire. The officer stood, ready to board his ship. High above them men on the *Westy* were looking down and cheering. Adam searched their faces, looking for his father, but they were too far away to be seen clearly. He scrambled up the ladder after the officer.

On the main deck, Adam ran one way, then the other. "Pelko," he kept saying. "Lieutenant Pelko?"

The sailors looked at him blankly and kept going.

Adam ran through dark, narrow passageways, down ladders, then up ladders. The ship shook. Adam was blown through a doorway. A hail of debris clattered down around him. Boulders seemed to be bouncing across the decks. Men were screaming. Everything was loose and coming apart. The noise was deafening, as if the ship were being sledgehammered to pieces.

In a passageway a sailor with an ax tore open a locked ammunition trunk. A box was thrust into Adam's hands, and he was ordered to follow the man ahead of him. Out on the deck, next to a gun pod, a colored sailor crouched over twin machine guns, shooting at the attacking planes. The deck shook. Adam dropped the box. Pieces of the ship and pieces of men rained down around him. A foot. An arm. He saw everything through a red haze. He ran. He slipped in blood. The launch was still at the foot of the ladder, and he fled the ship.

The launch was stalled. The coxswain, a stump of cigar in his mouth, was frantically working on the engine. "Kid," he shouted as Adam jumped in the boat, "get me that wrench." It was as if he'd been waiting for Adam, not for who he really was, but for who they thought he was—a sailor. And maybe he was a sailor, at least for now. Whatever he was, he wasn't what he'd been this morning.

The launch crew worked on the engine. The boat was sitting directly under a massive anchor that shook every time a bomb fell. Finally the engine started and they moved away looking for survivors.

As they passed port side to the overturned *Oklahoma* a man escaped from an underwater porthole and shot to the surface like a seal, hair slicked back, eyes huge. He wouldn't get into the boat, but, dog paddling, kept turning to his ship, saying his mates were down there and he'd wait for them. Berman, the coxswain, cut the throttle and sat there, talking to the guy. Nobody else came out of the ship, but the man still wouldn't get in the launch, and they left him.

The harbor was dotted with small boats picking up men who had leaped from the burning ships. Oil was everywhere: tarlike floating islands on the surface of the water. Adam worked alongside Rinaldi, the sailor who had pulled him into the launch. He was a cocky fireplug of a guy. He'd point to someone in the water, and then they'd throw out lines or a life buoy or one of the long boat hooks. The men came out of the water black with oil, sometimes only their eyes showing. Adam looked at each man. Any one of them could have been his father.

Some men refused help and swam toward shore. Some men they brought to the boat were burned so badly they could hardly be touched. Adam reached to help a man into the boat and skin came off in his hand. He gagged, then vomited over the side. Ashamed, he looked at Rinaldi. "That's okay, buddy," Rinaldi said.

Men flopped and twisted on the deck, barely able to speak. A man with a terrible wound in his side kept thanking them and telling them that he had to get back to his ship.

Berman never stopped chewing on an unlit cigar, and he never stopped cursing. First he cursed the Japs. Then he cursed the Americans—the admirals and generals and the high command. Why hadn't they known the attack was coming? How did they let it happen? Where was the admiral—sitting on his fanny, drinking tea? Get him over here, let him see this! He'd like to stick his face in it!

One man with huge tattooed arms hung on the edge of the boat. His face was black with oil. "Boys," he said. He was looking at Adam, nodding at him as if he knew him. "Good boys," he said. And then he just slid away under the water, went down and didn't come up.

Nothing in Adam's life had prepared him for any of this. Not for the maimed, not for the wounded. Not for the dead they left floating in the water. He'd read about war. He'd imagined himself in a war, but never like this. War was a fight between equals. It was clean. It was fair. The best man won. But this—what was it? There were no words that he'd ever learned, no book that he'd ever read, that had prepared him for this. What was it? It was stink and blood and dying.

When the launch couldn't hold any more survivors, they headed for the docks. At Ford Island, the men who could, walked off. The others were carried off on stretchers.

The naval air station was wrecked, the hangars burned down to the girders. Every one of the PBYs that Adam had always thought looked like flying dolphins had been hit and were strewn like trash across the field. Survivors kept coming off the boats and crawling out of the water. They were in rags. They were naked. They were covered with oil.

Rinaldi was guiding a man who had been blinded by oil. Adam ran ahead to find a medic. The medics were running from man to man. Adam finally got one to stop. The medic pointed to a building on the other side of the field. "If your man can walk, take him there."

They were almost to the emergency hospital when the warning siren wailed. The three of them dropped down behind a wall. Near them, sailors were pulling machine guns out of wrecked planes and setting them up. The siren kept wailing, but no planes came, no bombs fell. "Let's move on, buddy," Rinaldi said.

The emergency hospital had been set up in a mess hall, a big, open room. The wounded were lying everywhere, on tables and on the floor. The dead were stacked up under a window.

Adam walked through the room, looking at each man, looking for his father. The wounded called out to him for water. He found a sink and filled Dixie cups, glad for something to do.

14

"Where do you guys think you're going?" A marine sergeant stopped Rinaldi and Adam as they left the building. He was clean. He was neat. He was in uniform. He had a gun strapped around his waist.

"You're a marine," Rinaldi said, "but we're navy."

"You're marines now. If you can walk and hold a gun, you're a marine." He pointed to a group of men. "Over there with the rest of the volunteers."

Rinaldi looked at Adam and shrugged. The sergeant blew his whistle. "Line up! Let's look like something! Whatever you were, you're a marine now. I know you're a bunch of cooks and clerks. You probably thought you were working in a country club, but this is war, and we're forming a fighting company."

All the time the sergeant was talking, Adam was watching the smudgy sky. Navy antiaircraft guns were firing. The noise—the chatter and boom—was continuous.

"First thing we do is clean up." The sergeant didn't talk. He yelled. "I want you looking like marines. Follow me! On the double!" He ran, and they all ran after him.

Adam stayed glued to Rinaldi. Even if he wanted to, he didn't know how he could tell Rinaldi that he didn't belong here.

Once they found out that he was just a kid, they'd throw him out. Maybe. Or maybe they needed bodies. Better to say nothing, anyway. As long as he was here, there was a chance he might find his father.

The sergeant set them loose in a navy barracks. "Clean up and find clothes. Take what you need. You don't have to pay for this."

The barracks had been ransacked already, footlockers emptied, clothes, bedding, books, bottles—everything thrown on the floor. They found towels, but there was no running water, and all they could do was smear around the oil on their skin.

"This needs paint thinner," Rinaldi said, rummaging through a footlocker. He found a bottle of Aqua Velva aftershave lotion. "This is going to do it," he said, dousing himself with it, then passing it to Adam.

He threw a blue work shirt to Adam. "What happened to your back, buddy? It looks like you went through barbed wire."

"Bullet," Adam said.

"It just skinned you," Rinaldi said. "Lucky."

Adam scrubbed at the oil on his arms, and the whole mystery of the day came over him. Look where he was! Here in this barracks, covered with oil, wearing someone else's work shirt and pants. He didn't know why he was here. It was like the army song—he was here because he was here. That was it. When he thought about the day—was it only a day?—it was as if everything that had happened had to happen.

The shirt mostly fit, except the sleeves were short. The

pants were okay. He found socks, but there were no boots, and he put on a pair of black dress shoes.

Rinaldi stuck a sailor cap squarely on Adam's head. "The official look, buddy." Rinaldi's cap was pushed to the back of his head. Adam had a quick look at himself in a mirror, then pushed his cap back like Rinaldi's.

Rinaldi nodded. "Now you look like something."

They had hardly stepped outside when the sirens went berserk again. He and Rinaldi dove into a drainage ditch and waited for bombs that didn't come. Adam's face was in the dirt. He had that sweet Aqua Velva smell all over him. He giggled. He couldn't stop giggling, and he didn't understand why. This wasn't a funny place, nothing funny was going on, but he couldn't stop. Maybe it was because he was alive. He'd been shot and he'd just kept going, like a cartoon, like Popeye the Sailor Man. Nothing could stop him.

Or maybe he was laughing because now he was a sailor. Did you become a sailor just by putting on a uniform? Not in the ordinary, regular world. But everything today was turned inside out. So maybe he was laughing for no reason, because this was a world without reason. Next to him Rinaldi started laughing too.

"All right, you guys, what's the joke?" The sergeant was above them. "Let's go! Look alive!"

Adam jumped to his feet, and he and Rinaldi fell in with the others.

"Dress right. Dress left. Left turn! Forward . . . march!"

They marched double time. They ran. Adam stumbled into

the man in front of him, stepped on his heels and was cursed. Rinaldi rolled his eyes in sympathy.

They marched to the marine armory, where they were each given a rifle, a .30 caliber bolt-action Springfield, complete with a sling. Some of the men acted like they'd never seen a gun before. Adam knew about .22s, but this gun weighed a ton. He sighted it, getting the feel of it. He watched Rinaldi loading the clip and did the same. Then he set the safety and slung the rifle over his shoulder.

The sergeant marched them to the beach, counted off ten men, and left them there on guard. Everyone else loaded onto a launch, and they headed across the harbor toward the main gate. The enemy planes were gone, but the AA guns were still firing. When they passed the *Oklahoma*, rescue operations were in progress. Workmen with burning torches were cutting holes in the hull trying to reach the sailors trapped inside. But there were no workmen, no rescue operations on the *Arizona*, which seemed to have sunk even deeper into the bay. Only its flag still fluttered on the stern. Once Adam had climbed all over that ship, and his father had showed him off. All those men who had lined the decks, the sailors and the officers standing at attention in their gleaming white uniforms . . . where were they now?

For a while nobody talked. Then they started, one sailor after another, and it was the same story over and over.

"When the planes came, I was in the sack."

"I was having my first cup of java."

"I had my whites on, I was on my way to church."

"I was sitting in the head with my pants down."

"This is history, you men," the sergeant said. "You're going to tell this to your kids, if you live that long, so look sharp. There's an enemy out there. The Jap planes could come back anytime."

Everyone began to talk again. The scuttlebutt flew.

"The Japs can land anywhere they want . . . who's to stop them?"

"They could be in Honolulu right now, kissing their Jap cousins."

"I heard they landed paratroopers on the Punchbowl."

The Punchbowl. Adam thought about his sister and his mother alone in that little house. The talk about the Japs, the Japs, the Japs made him sick, but when he thought about his father, he wanted to kill, too. His nerves were shaved razor thin.

15

The main gate was a mob scene. Traffic was backed up both ways, and civilian workers, most of them Japanese, crowded around every vehicle that came through, demanding rides and blocking the road.

"Everybody back!" the sergeant bellowed. "Clear the gate! Back! Back!" He formed the squad into a line, and with rifles raised, they began pressing the crowd away from the gate.

People gave ground, but they were angry. "Why are you doing this?" they shouted. "We're not the enemy!"

"Where are the buses?"

"Bombs are falling on Honolulu!"

"We have to get home."

Once the gate was cleared, vehicles began to move again, and the sergeant took Rinaldi and a couple of other men to unload machine guns from a truck. He left an old guy, Tom, a supply sergeant, in charge.

"Boys, spread out a little," Tom said. "You heard the sarge. We got to keep an eye on these people."

Adam took a position along the edge of the road, rifle at the ready. From the moment he'd heard about the Japanese paratroopers on the Punchbowl, Adam knew he had to go home. Every few minutes he took a few more steps away from the gate. With every step he asked himself if he was right to leave. What would his father say? *You're deserting your post!* And what about Rinaldi and the sergeant? He kept taking steps. He knew it wasn't wrong to worry about his mother and sister . . . but was he just making excuses for himself?

He kept looking back, but nobody was watching him, and he moved farther and farther away from the gate. Beside him, a truck was rolling slowly along. "You going to Honolulu?" Adam called through the open window. The driver was Japanese. He could almost have been Davi's older brother. He had that same sleepy look.

"Honolulu, yeah," the driver said. The cab and the back of the truck were packed with people. "Hop on, sailor. I could use an armed guard. I don't know what I'm going to find up ahead."

Adam was up and in the back of the truck in a second. It was a piece of luck. The civilians made room for him. "What ship you on, sailor?" a woman asked. She was wearing dungarees, a shirt, and a bright kerchief tied under her chin.

Adam hesitated for a moment. "The *Westy*," he said.

One man—he was no taller than Adam—kept looking at the gun, then at Adam, with a kind of considering look, as if he knew Adam was only a make-believe sailor. Adam frowned and turned away, as if he had more important business.

The highway was jammed with vehicles, and they stopped a lot. Every time the traffic started moving again, the people in back yelled at the driver to go. "Go! Go! Move!" And each time, the driver stuck his hand out the window and waved, and said, "Hold your horses, people."

"Hey, sailor," he called to Adam. They were stopped again. "Stand in front, by the cab. You see a Jap plane, bang on the top."

"I'm watching," Adam said, his eyes on the horizon. Guarding the truck was important too. He watched the sky. If an enemy plane appeared, he would bang as hard as he could on the cab. He would alert everybody. He would save them.

It was close to the middle of the day, and the sky was like a hot blue plate. Birds darting through the trees set his heart pumping. One minute he was leaning against the top of the cab, watching birds, and the next a Japanese fighter plane, a Zero that seemed bigger than the whole sky, was on top of them.

Adam banged on the cab. People tumbled off the truck. Then he had the gun to his shoulder. How that happened, how he got to the top of the cab, he didn't remember, but he was up there, shooting as fast as he could, one clip after another.

The empty shells bounced off the cab. He was excited, so excited that he was trembling. It was the smell of gunpowder and the way the rifle recoiled into his shoulder. He kept shooting, even after the plane had disappeared.

"Hey!" The driver was looking up at him. "What are you doing up there?" People were coming out of the ditches. "It's gone," the driver said. "Get down."

Adam slid off the cab and jumped down into the road. His head was on fire, and his heart, too. He walked along the side of the road with the gun raised, at the ready. They passed a car with all the windows shot out, and, once, there was gunfire ahead. He put the gun to his shoulder several times, but there were no more planes.

For a while he and the truck kept pace, but then the truck got ahead of him. "Come on," the driver called, sticking his head out the window. "Come on, hop on."

Adam waved and kept walking. He was still too keyed up to get back on the truck.

16

Adam walked. Sun high, almost no shade anywhere, the sky as blank as a sheet of paper, as if smoke and planes—the attack itself—had been erased. Here and there cars had been abandoned. He heard more firing, sometimes a distant explosion like thunder. Once, he saw a plane falling, spinning out of control. Maybe it was the plane he'd fired at. A thin spiral of smoke appeared over the trees. It reminded him of summers camping in the mountains and the way smoke from their campfire drifted up through the branches.

Looking for a place to relieve himself, Adam turned off on a dirt road where a hubcap was nailed to a tree. That was when he saw the jeep sitting in a bamboo grove with the key in the ignition.

"Hello?" he called, hoping to get a ride. "Anyone home?" When nobody appeared, he began to think something had happened to the driver. He poked around in the bushes, calling, making a lot of noise.

"Hello, hello?" He looked the jeep over. No blood. No bullet holes. He got in the driver's seat, put the gun down next to him, and worked the shift through the gears. He could drive this jeep. He pulled the choke out, pushed it in, then turned on the key. The engine light came on. He found the starter on the floor. The engine coughed a couple of times, then caught.

He drove the jeep forward a few feet, then back. He blew the horn. "Last chance," he said, and blew the horn some more. Then he drove the jeep down the dirt road. Not a car or another person around. Nothing but sugarcane fields on both sides.

He passed low buildings and warehouses. He kept both hands on the wheel, not rushing, looking around, imagining the jeep was his. Then, ahead, in the middle of the road, he saw a man wearing bright blue coveralls and what looked like a white parachute harness. The man came running toward the jeep. Adam's mouth dried. *Jap paratrooper,* he thought. He meant to put the car in reverse, but he forgot everything and pressed hard on the accelerator.

The car leaped forward. It was running away with him. He was going straight for the man, who jumped aside, shouting. "Are you drunk? You almost killed me."

Adam hit the brake and the jeep skidded off the road. He sat there, trembling. He couldn't move. He could hardly speak.

The man came up to the jeep and stared menacingly at Adam. "Who are you?"

"Adam . . ." he stammered. "Adam Pelko."

"Pelko?" The man looked at the gun and then at Adam. "Kind of an exciting day today, right, Pelko?"

Adam nodded. "I thought . . . you know . . . you were in the middle of the road, and—"

"You got a cigarette, Pelko?"

Adam shook his head.

"I smoked every one of mine. You sure you haven't got one? I'm dying for a smoke."

"No, sir."

"You don't have to 'sir' me. I'm the same as you. I'm Brown and you're Pelko. Where you going, Pelko?"

"Honolulu."

"Okay, you got company."

They pushed the jeep back onto the road. Adam was still shaken up, and he asked Brown if he wanted to drive.

"No sweat. But how about you put that gun in back?"

Adam put the rifle and the bandolier in the backseat, then got in on the passenger side. As Brown drove he got more and more talkative. He was based at Hickman Field, ground crew, and this morning—"of all mornings," he said—he'd gone up for a ride with a pilot friend.

"Joy ride. Some joy. The next thing we know, there're planes flying with us, and this Jap pilot is looking at me and I'm looking at him, and the next thing I know, we get hit. I wasn't even going to put the parachute on. 'What do I need that for,' I said to my friend. All the jumping I do, I do on the ground. And he says, 'Put it on, Brown, or stay on the ground.' He saved my life." Brown fell silent. "I don't think he got out."

17

In the middle of the afternoon they drove into Honolulu. For some time the engine had been misfiring, but Brown kept it going, playing with the choke and the gas pedal. He didn't want to stop, and neither did Adam.

Honolulu was like a battlefield. Military everywhere. Marines on the roof of the telephone building, army trucks in the streets, even a tank.

On Hotel Street the jeep died. They pushed it to the curb. Brown put his head under the hood and began to fiddle with the engine. This was the street with all the honky-tonks and bars, the street Adam's parents had warned him against. Now it swarmed with military vehicles and military police. Adam kept an eye on the MPs, afraid they'd notice him. *What's your unit, sailor? Where'd you get the jeep? And that gun?*

For a while he stood looking into the window of an army-navy store, where sailors and soldiers came to buy their insignias and get them sewn onto their uniforms. He felt trapped, impatient to keep going, to get home. "Any luck?"

"I'm giving up," Brown said, slamming down the hood and kicking the jeep a couple of times. "Let's go over to the Y. We'll catch a ride back to the base."

"I'm going that way," Adam said, pointing in the opposite direction.

Brown shrugged. "Suit yourself. See you around sometime." And he walked off.

Adam took the gun. He wanted it, but he was afraid that he'd be noticed. In the doorway of an empty store he took off his shirt and wrapped the gun and bandolier in it and put them under his arm.

Once he left the downtown, everything changed. He passed from one tree-lined street to another. It was another world, a world without bombs. It was too peaceful, too quiet, too ordinary. He kept waiting for an explosion, for gunfire. He stayed close to buildings, looking up, ready to take cover. A car honked and his heart jumped. A door slamming sent him crouching under a hedge.

On every street and on every corner people were gathered, talking. Cars on lawns were being loaded with boxes and bedding. A boy on a bicycle sped by, yelling, "Don't drink the water. I heard it on the radio. It's poisoned."

Adam heard people talking about curfews and blackouts. "Sailor," a man called out. Adam checked to see if his cap was on right. "Sailor, are the roads open?"

"Jammed."

Trees were casting long shadows when he turned up Punchbowl Street. He was close to home now, and he started running. Darkness closed in. Near the house he hid the gun in the bushes, then shook out the shirt and put it on.

18

The house was dark. The front door was locked. Adam went to the back. The kitchen door was locked too. He tried the windows. Locked and curtained. Where were they? Had they left without him? Had something happened? He went around to the front again, yelling now and banging on the door. "Mom! Bea! Mom!"

The door opened a crack. "Who are you?" a voice whispered.

"Where's my mother?" He tried to push into the house. It was his house! "Where's my sister? Who are you!"

"Shhh!" A light flickered. He saw the shadow of a face.

"Who are you?" he said again.

Then another voice—a voice he recognized—said, "It's Adam. Let him in, Janet."

It was Mrs. Parker, their neighbor, and the woman holding the door against him was another neighbor, Mrs. Collins.

"Oh, it's Adam," she said. She was holding a golf club like a weapon. "All that shouting, it sounded like Japanese to us, Adam." She was still whispering. "We've been hearing so many things on the radio—"

Mrs. Parker pushed her aside. "Janet," she hissed, "will you stop telling him stories and let him in? Go tell Marilyn her son is home. Our little hero is back."

"Is something wrong?" he said. "Is Mom okay?"

"She's putting Bea in her pajamas." Mrs. Parker tugged his arm. "She's been worried sick about you, Adam."

He stumbled going into the living room. It was crowded with women and children, some of them holding shovels and sticks. It was so spooky. A flashlight played over the ceiling. Everything suddenly seemed unfamiliar, as if he'd been away for so long he'd forgotten where he lived and had walked into the wrong house.

Then Bea came flying at him, and his mother was there, too, grabbing him and holding him so tight it hurt.

"Where were you?" she said. "All day, this whole terrible day, I've been waiting. I've been waiting to hear from you. Bombs falling, your father out there, and you, God only knows where." She pushed him away. "Do you know what kind of day this has been for me?" She sank down in a chair.

"Mom." He didn't know how to explain, even how to begin to explain. "I'm sorry, Mom."

"Sorry . . . ," she said.

He picked up Bea and held on to her. "Did you eat your candy?" A dumb thing to say, but it was all he could think of.

"I saved you a bite. You're a sailor?" She took his cap off and put it on her head.

His mother was sitting there, her hand over her mouth. "Mom . . . I'm sorry." He looked around helplessly. He wanted to tell her everything, that he'd been shot and about his father's ship, but he couldn't. Not now. "What are all these people doing here, Mom?"

"We're defending ourselves." She picked up a hammer from the floor. "Ridiculous, isn't it? Adam, you smell! What is that?"

"Probably oil," he said.

"Oil? Where were you?"

"I'll tell you . . ." He was so tired now, he couldn't speak. He just managed to scrub up and change clothes, and then he fell on his bed.

He didn't think he'd slept at all, but when he woke up, all the other people had left. Bea was asleep, and his mother was sitting in the dark on one of Bea's little chairs by the front door.

He sat down on the floor next to her. The door was open, and they watched the flashes of gunfire and tracers, like shooting stars in the sky. After a while she said, "Now, tell me where you were all day."

"I started out fishing," he said.

"Fishing! You didn't say that in your note."

"I went with Davi—you know, that boy from my class?"

"The Japanese boy?"

"Yes."

"All right. Then what? Were you fishing the whole day?"

"We went to Pearl Harbor."

"Pearl Harbor?" It took her only a moment to absorb it. "Pearl Harbor! You were there?"

All day he'd been pretty steady. Well, he'd vomited once. Now, though, with his mother's hand on his shoulder, his voice trembled, and it made him angry. He didn't want to break down. "Yes," he said. "Yes, we were at Pearl. We were on the water when it began."

He wanted to tell her everything, wanted her to admire him, how he'd seen so much, so many terrible things. But he kept hearing his father saying, *Not in front of your mother.* There were things in the world, things that happened, that you didn't talk about in front of women.

He tried to sort out what he could say and what he shouldn't say. "We found a rowboat," he began. Then he couldn't stop. It all came out—almost all—how they were in the water when the attack began, and the torpedo bombers and Martin's wound, and how Davi got beaten. He stopped, thinking about how he'd tried to push Davi out of the boat. How could he tell his mother that?

His mother was smoking, something she rarely did. "Go on," she said. "I know anyway. I'm not going to fall apart."

So he told her about the ships on fire, the *Oklahoma* tipped over, and how he was on the *West Virginia* when the bombing started again, and about the launch and the men they'd fished out of the harbor. He didn't speak about the *Arizona*. He knew what he'd seen, but by not saying the words, he could almost believe—he could hope—that it might still not be true.

"And what about your father's ship?" she said. "Did you see it?" And again she said, "I know. I saw the planes. Everybody in Honolulu knows what happened. The whole fleet is gone."

"Not the whole fleet."

"Your father—his ship is gone."

"Mom, we don't know anything for sure. There were a lot of survivors. Dad could have been on another ship—he could be all right."

"All right?" she said and closed her eyes for a moment. "You're right. I won't know anything for sure until I hear it from the navy."

It was only later, when he asked her to look at his back, that she broke down. "What is this?" she cried.

"It's only a scratch, Mom."

"No, your back is really bruised." The peroxide she dabbed on his wound stung and he winced. "Sorry," she said. "How did this happen, Adam? I want to know."

"Mom, don't get upset. It was a bullet. They strafed the rowboat and—"

"A bullet. They shot you?" She started crying. "I can't stand it. I just can't stand it."

19

It was a long night. Pink tracers arced across the sky. The gunfire never stopped. What was frightening was not knowing who was shooting, and where. The least sound, just the rustling of the palms, and Adam could almost see the enemy creeping toward them. He went outside to retrieve his gun. The moon lit his way. There were no lights anywhere. The city was blacked out. It was as if Honolulu had vanished.

When he came back, he sat down next to his mother by the open door and showed her the gun and the clip. "Be careful," she said as he loaded it. "Set the safety."

"I know."

"I know you know." She sighed. "Your father taught you right. But I'm nervous. I don't want the gun sitting around out in the open."

"Okay, Mom." He went to his room and put the gun on the high shelf in the closet, then told his mother where it was. She was smoking again. "Give me a puff." He reached for her cigarette.

"Since when do you smoke?" she said, but she let him take it. "Don't let the lit end show, or we'll have the air-raid warden." They sat there passing the cigarette back and forth.

"Adam, you should go lie down again," she said. "You don't even realize how tired you are."

He lay down near the open doorway on the floor, next to her. Outside the long leathery leaves of the banana tree chattered in the wind. Adam couldn't get comfortable, but his mother was here, and he didn't want to leave her. Images flickered through his mind with the rapidity of a movie projector. Water . . . ships . . . a boat rocking . . . men like fish beneath the water . . .

He awoke abruptly, sat up, his whole body tense. His mother had thrown a blanket over him. The moon was down, the clouds had disappeared, and high up he saw the cold, distant stars.

"Awake?" his mother said. She had made tea and brought it out on a tray with soda crackers and jam. "It's Monday morning," she said. "It's tomorrow. We may know something in a few hours. I think your father will get a message to us. I think he's alive. I feel it."

"Yes," he said. He knew it was true. He believed it. He could already hear the phone ringing and his father's voice. *Adam, I'm not hurt bad. How are you kids? Let me talk to your mother.*

In the distance a dog barked, and then birds began to sing as if it were just another day. Bea was singing to herself in her room. "A tisket, a tasket, a little yellow basket . . ."

His mother began making breakfast. "Turn on the radio," she said. "It's almost time for the mainland broadcast."

Adam went into the living room, where the radio, a floor model, sat next to his father's chair. He turned the sound up loud enough for his mother to hear in the kitchen, then went back.

"Want me to do something?" he said.

"You can make the orange juice."

He took the glass juice squeezer from the cupboard, cut six

oranges in half, and lined them up, then began squeezing them, one at a time. He was only half listening to the radio. Then his mother exclaimed, "Adam, listen! It's President Roosevelt."

"Yesterday, December 7, 1941 . . ." The president's voice, slow and measured, filled the house. To Adam, it seemed to come from somewhere higher, as if God himself were speaking to them. "—a date which will live in infamy—the United States of America was suddenly and deliberately attacked by naval and air forces of the Empire of Japan."

His mother sat down, and Adam stood behind her, his hands on her shoulders. Adam listened intently. He would never forget this, not a word, not a breath. He imagined the president— his metal-rimmed glasses, that long, kind face—sitting, his legs covered by a blanket, his little dog Fala next to him. He seemed to speak directly to Adam.

"The attack yesterday on the Hawaiian islands caused severe damage to American naval and military forces. Very many American lives have been lost."

It was true. Adam knew it. He had seen the bodies floating in the water. He knew it, but now the president had said it and everyone knew it.

His mother was silent. She sat listening, her head bowed. He felt so sorry for her, so sorry for himself, for them all. They stayed that way, not moving, listening to President Roosevelt to the very end.

"I ask that the Congress declare that since the unprovoked and dastardly attack by Japan on Sunday, December 7, a state of war has existed between the United States and the Japanese empire."

20

Those next days were strange and agonizingly long, not because so much happened, but because almost nothing happened. They were waiting. The radio was on all day, and his mother was on the phone constantly, talking to the other navy wives. "Rumors," she told Adam. "That's all I'm hearing."

"Scuttlebutt," he said.

She nodded. "Not a single fact."

What was fact was that they were at war, and the army had taken control, and martial law was in effect throughout the islands. Everything was closed—banks, schools, government offices. There was a call for blood donors and his mother had gone. All true facts. And it was true that workmen were cutting holes in the bottom of the *Oklahoma*, searching for men trapped inside. Every story he and his mother heard about a rescue lifted their spirits.

But the other stuff—the stories about the Japanese civilians in Hawaii, that they were using their cars to block traffic on the Kamehameha Highway, and that fishermen were signaling to a Japanese fleet off the coast, and that Japanese paratroopers had already landed—all rumors.

The one that got his mother laughing was the barking dog

story—dogs trained to bark in Morse code, sending messages to offshore Japanese submarines.

"Do you believe anyone could take that seriously? We're like a bunch of headless chickens," his mother said. "Of course, they could land, but how are they going to support a landing force? How are they going to keep ammunition and supplies coming? It's too far. Too far fetched. An air strike is one thing, but this . . ."

She sounded like his father giving one of his lectures on military strategy and the iron rules of war. She had that look now. If you wanted to convince her, you better make sense.

That first morning, Mrs. Parker had come flying through the hedge separating their houses to tell them that she'd heard from her husband. "I spoke to him, Marilyn. He's okay. He wasn't on his ship." She was so excited she could hardly breathe. "He was at headquarters when it started. Didn't get a scratch. He watched the whole thing from a window."

"Wonderful," Adam's mother said.

Mrs. Parker's expression changed. "Marilyn, maybe it's a sign. I told him to find out about Emory. You'll have good news too, very soon, I know you will."

"Wonderful," his mother said again.

If there was ever a tear, if his mother had cried, she wiped it before he could see. "We don't know," she kept saying to Adam. "We won't know anything for sure till the navy tells us. And not a word to Bea."

But not once did Bea ask about their father; she was used to his being away. Who she missed was Koniko, who had disappeared after the attack. "When is she coming?" Bea asked. "Who's going to play with me? Adam, will you play with me?" She handed him a ballerina costume to put on one of her paper dolls. "You didn't do it right," she said. "Not like Koniko. Where's Koniko, Mama?"

"The buses aren't running this week," his mother said, giving Adam a warning look. "Koniko will come soon."

An airplane went over, and they stopped and listened. "Not Japanese," Bea said, looking at Adam.

"Smart kid," he said. "Sticky brain." And he thought about Davi—and Martin, too. Were they okay? He wanted to see them, but he didn't want to leave his mother. She might hear something about his father. Adam would see Davi when he went back to school, but school stayed closed. Everything had changed.

He was sleeping in his mother's room now, on the folding cot by the door. He kept the rifle underneath the cot.

"Why are you sleeping here?" Bea asked the first night.

"I'm guarding you."

"You're the guard dog?"

"Mr. Guard Dog to you."

Bea giggled. She had the best giggle. She could always make him laugh. That hadn't changed.

A week after the attack Adam went looking for Hideko's shovel in the garden shed. He was rested—and restless—and needed to do something. In the garden he began digging an air-raid shelter, one of the things they'd been encouraged to do. The digging was harder than he expected and he stopped a lot. Leaning on the shovel, he lost himself watching the shadows of the palm leaves darting back and forth on the roof.

Davi was the first person he'd ever met who talked about light. Adam had never thought about it before Davi. He had never thought about air, either, and being able to breathe. But was there anything better than breath? He remembered Martin and the stick in his chest and the way it had moved with every breath.

And then he thought about his father trapped inside the *Arizona*, him and all those men in that suffocating darkness. He filled his lungs. He breathed. He breathed again. He couldn't get enough air.

21

"I thought you were dead," Davi said. He was in the work yard, where his father had fixed Adam's bike.

Some greeting, after Adam had come to see him.

"I thought you were dead." He said it again.

"No such luck." Adam turned the navy cap around on his head. He thought Davi might say something about it. He thought Davi would ask him what had happened to him. But Davi didn't say anything about anything.

"I thought you were dead," he said a third time. It wasn't funny the first time, and it didn't get any funnier. But Davi was smiling, and the smile kept growing.

"So, what happened?" Adam asked. "Is Martin okay?"

"What do you mean, 'okay'? He almost died! He's still in the hospital."

"Well, I didn't know. Did they get that stick out okay?"

"Stick? Stick! It was right in his heart, but what do you care. He's nothing, right? He's just a gook, yeah? We're all gooks, right?"

Adam slapped the navy cap against his leg. "What's going on with you?"

Davi shrugged and stood there, snapping off twigs and dropping them on the ground.

Adam tried again. "How about you? You look like you came through okay."

Davi snorted. "Oh, yeah, I'm great." He spun around, then made a couple of fancy jujitsu moves, finishing up with a kick that ended right under Adam's chin.

"Hell!" Adam jumped back. "What's with you, Davi?"

Davi kicked over the pile of twigs he'd made, then he kicked the wheel of a wagon.

"Is it something I did?" But he knew. "If it's about when we were in the boat—I'm sorry about that. I wasn't thinking straight."

"Sure you're sorry. Like my father says, 'Unfortunate situation.' Forget it."

Adam threw his cap down. "You want to hit me? Go on, slug me! Give it your best shot. Get it out!"

Davi looked at him. "The easy way."

"Listen, Davi"—Adam picked up his cap—"anybody can make a mistake. Unless they're perfect, like you," he added.

No laugh. No nothing. Davi just gave him that gimlet-eye look. "Yeah," he said, "my mistake is being Japanese."

"Aw, come on," Adam said. "It's not that way—"

"Not for you, it isn't. What do you know?" Davi pushed into Adam's face. "Do people say things when you walk down the street? Do they spit at you? Do they call you a filthy yellow Jap?"

"That stinks," Adam said.

"No kidding." Davi grabbed Adam's arm and held it next to his. "Look at you and look at me. Am I yellow? Are you white?

Clouds are white. Lemons are yellow. Why are all you haoles so stupid? I didn't attack Pearl Harbor."

"I never said you did."

Davi gave him a sarcastic smile. "Yeah, that wasn't you trying to throw me out of the boat."

"I told you I was sorry. You want me to say it again? I'm sorry. I'm sorry—"

"Shut up," Davi said abruptly, and walked away. Then he came back. "They took my father away."

"Your father—" Adam thought of that mild man who had fixed his bike and wouldn't take money from him. "Who took him away? Why?"

"Government men. Early in the morning. A bunch of big FBI haoles." Davi's face suddenly filled. "Told my father he had five minutes, and then he was gone. They didn't even give him time to get his toothbrush."

"It must be a mistake," Adam said. "Your father never did anything. Why would they do that?"

"He's Japanese, that's why. He lived in this country twenty years, and they wouldn't let him be a citizen. So he's Japanese. And because he went back to Japan a couple of times to see my uncles, they say he's a spy. Or he might be. They have him behind barbed wire on Sand Island."

"Davi, that's wrong. I don't believe in that stuff."

"I'm not mad at you," Davi said at last. "Not really. Not anymore. You know who I'm mad at? Japan, for starting this war. The empire of Japan! I hate them for that."

Adam nodded. "I'm sorry about your father." Now was the

time to tell Davi about his own father, but he didn't. He couldn't. He was suddenly feeling too sorry for himself even to talk about it. Because even though Davi's father wasn't home yet, at least they knew he was alive, and they knew where he was.

On the way to the hospital to see Martin they went through Davi's neighborhood. It took Adam a while to figure out why the narrow, crowded streets seemed different from the last time he'd been here. The streets were just as crowded with the same Japanese faces, but it was quieter now. There had been so much noise and color before. Now the banners and signs and Japanese things were all gone. No portraits of the emperor, no ceremonial samurai swords in the store windows. Even the women were different. They all wore dresses, Western style. No more kimonos and sandals. It was as if no one wanted to look Japanese anymore.

In his room Martin was sitting up in bed, the prince on his throne. His mother was there, serving him, and his father sat in the window, eating sunflower seeds and spitting the shells into his hands.

Martin didn't look sick. He looked happy. "Davi! Adam! Ma, you know Davi. This other guy is my haole friend, Adam. Never saw anyone row like him. Hug him, Ma. Davi, too, Ma."

His mother gave each of them a big squeeze and a kiss on the cheek. "My boy's friends. Good boys!"

Martin pulled the hospital gown open to show where they'd

stitched him up. "This close to my heart." He held two fingers together. "That close."

His mother put her hands over her ears. "I don't want to hear."

Martin wanted to compare wounds with Adam. "Show my parents where you got shot."

"I wasn't really shot," Adam said. "It only grazed me."

"What do you mean? You got it the same as me. A bullet hit you," Martin insisted. "Right, Davi?" He wouldn't stop until Adam had pulled up his shirt and everyone looked at his back. "See that, Ma? Bullets can't hurt this haole. Just bounced off. Pig god watching over him. Adam and Martin get the Purple Heart," Martin went on. "Davi? Nothing. You know why he wasn't shot. They looked down"—Martin craned his neck, as if he were a pilot, then made an airplane sound—"'Oooh, Davi Mori! Can't shoot my cousin.'"

"Shut up, Martin," Davi said. "Don't even joke about it."

But the next minute he was sitting next to Martin on the bed. Martin's father wanted to take their picture. "You sit on the other side, Adam," Martin said. "Okay, Pa!"

"Pretty face," his mother said. "Smile, boys."

22

Adam and his mother waited. That's all they were doing—waiting. Waiting to hear something. Waiting to hear from his father.

He woke up waiting and he went to sleep waiting.

Waiting. The clock ticking. *Tick, tick, tick, tick* . . . He couldn't get the sound out of his head. He hated it. But sometimes it seemed to stop, and then he couldn't breathe.

Every day now there was news, and it was never good. Every day they heard about ships destroyed, the number of wounded, the number of dead. The *Nevada* had run aground. The *Utah* had been sunk. The *Arizona* had gone down so fast the eight or nine hundred men belowdecks were lost in an instant.

The clock ticked. Every moment without word from his father was like a door closing.

Adam woke up one morning knowing he was going back to the base. He had heard his mother pacing the night before. He had to go back. He had to find out something. Anything. Anything would be better than this waiting and uncertainty.

He left his mother a note: GONE TO FIND OUT ABOUT DAD. DON'T WORRY. I WON'T DO ANYTHING STUPID.

He dressed in his blue navy work shirt and dungarees, and even put on the black navy dress shoes. The cap went on his head. His lucky cap. It worked for him right away—he caught a ride downtown with a newspaper truck.

At the main gate Adam had an idea he would just walk through, that his cap and shirt would identify him, but the marine guards were stopping everyone. "ID," the guard said, holding out his hand.

"My father's in there." Adam said.

"I don't care who's in there. ID."

"My father's in there," Adam repeated. "Please. Can I go in?"

"You got a valid ID or not?"

"He was on the *Arizona*."

"Ah." The guard raised his hands. "Listen, kid, I can't do anything for you."

"Lieutenant Pelko," Adam said, still hoping.

"Sorry, sailor," the guard said.

Adam waited. The guards changed and he tried again. He hung around the gate all day, hoping he'd see someone he knew—maybe Rinaldi or the sergeant or even the officer from the *West Virginia*.

A Chinese man with cameras around his neck went in and out a few times. Everyone seemed to know him. Nobody asked *him* for his ID. Once, he stopped and took pictures of the gate and the guards. He was on a three-wheeled motor bike and wore a pith helmet. Around noon he brought sandwiches to the guards, and he brought one over to Adam, too.

"Thanks," Adam said. He hadn't even known he was hungry.

"You're waiting for someone?" the man asked.

"I'm trying to find out about my father. He was on the *Arizona*. Can you get me in?"

The man was peering through his camera, and he looked up. "I'll ask," he said. He went to the gate and talked to the guard. The guard looked over at Adam and shook his head.

A couple of times Adam thought of just making a dash for it. Maybe the rowboat was on the shore somewhere, waiting for him. He saw himself finding it, rowing out to the *Arizona*. . . . Crazy thoughts.

He tried the guard once more. "Do you know the marine sergeant who was here that Sunday? I was with him." He pointed to the sandbags and the guns near the entrance. "We did that. I'm looking for that sergeant. He'll tell you I'm okay. He'll remember me."

"What's his name?"

"I don't know. He had a big voice, though, shouted a lot."

The guard snorted. "That describes every sergeant in the marines. You better just stand back."

It was getting dark when Adam gave up and went home.

After two weeks Koniko returned to work. She wore a white dress, not her kimono, but she brought flowers the way she always did. "Mrs. Pelko, I feel shame to come."

"Oh, Koniko, no. Why do you say that?"

"Because of the Japanese attack," she said.

"Koniko," his mother said. "We missed you. We're glad you're back."

*   *   *

"Which is your father's ship?" Davi said. They were on the heights, looking down at Pearl Harbor. They had come back to get their bikes.

Adam pointed. There was almost nothing left to see of the *Arizona*, just a little of the superstructure sticking out of the water.

This was the first time Adam had seen the harbor since the day of the attack. Smoke still rose from the bay, but it was like the smoke you might see coming from a chimney. The harbor was cold and distant, and eerily quiet.

"We haven't heard anything from my father," Adam said.

Davi looked at him. "Nothing? You don't know anything?"

Adam shook his head.

"Maybe you'll hear something soon."

"Maybe," Adam said, and then anger gripped him.

He was angry that he'd said it. He was angry because he knew it wasn't true. He'd been kidding himself. He'd been praying, hoping, believing, agreeing with his mother, that they would still hear from his father. But he knew better. It had been too long. He'd been there. He'd seen the bodies floating in the bay. He'd seen the *Arizona*. He knew. Half the crew was still down there, buried, entombed. Dead.

He said it to himself again. *Dead.* His father had been taken from him. He was at the bottom of the harbor, in the *Arizona*. And it didn't make any sense. It would never make any sense.

23

A Western Union boy rode up on his bike and handed Adam's mother a telegram. She sat down and started to open the yellow envelope. Then she said, "You open it, Adam."

He took the envelope. He'd seen these yellow envelopes before: birthday greetings to his mother from her sister in Wisconsin came every year, and on his parents' anniversary there were always telegrams from their friends. There was something special about a telegram, something important and urgent, something that couldn't be denied.

He opened the envelope and took out the folded yellow sheet. The blue letters were pasted down on the paper in long strips.

THE SECRETARY OF WAR DESIRES ME TO EXPRESS HIS DEEP REGRET THAT YOUR HUSBAND LT EMORY J PELKO HAS BEEN MISSING IN ACTION AT PEARL HARBOR SINCE 7 DECEMBER 41 CONFIRMING LETTER FOLLOWS J A ULIO THE ADJUTANT GENERAL

The words wavered and seemed as big as alphabet blocks. "Read it to me," his mother said.

"The Secretary of War—" he read, and it was as if he were in school, aware of the sound of his voice, the words coming out automatically, one after another. "—desires me to express his deep regret that your husband, Lt. Emory J. Pelko, has been missing in action at Pearl Harbor since seven December forty-one. Confirming letter follows. J. A. Ulio, the Adjutant General."

"Missing in action," his mother said. She sat there, lips pressed together, hands crossed and gripping her shoulders. "Missing in action," she repeated.

Missing in action . . . that meant maybe. It meant there was still a chance. It meant there was still a little bit of hope.

But he knew. There was no hope.

When Adam's mother told him that the navy was sending all dependent families back to the mainland, his first thought was no, he wouldn't go. No! He wouldn't leave his father. He couldn't. The thought of leaving his father here at the bottom of Pearl Harbor was too awful.

But where was he going to live? He could hear his mother saying it. *How are you going to get along? Who's going to make your meals?*

He'd live with Davi, sleep in his room. He'd eat with the family, find a job so he could pay them, and he and Davi would go to school together.

"Mom—" She was packing a trunk, emptying the shelves in the hall closet. "Mom, I'm going to stay here," Adam said.

"What does that mean?" She handed him several blankets. "Put these in the trunk."

"I'm staying here in Hawaii," he said. "I want to."

His mother became very still. She seemed to grow taller and ominous. "Do you really think I'd leave you here, Adam? Why would I do that?"

"Why not? You're leaving Dad." He hadn't meant to say it that way. It came out sounding so brutal. And when he tried to explain, he made it worse. "Dad's here, we're leaving him," he cried. "We're abandoning him!"

"You know we don't have a choice. We're in the navy." She took the blankets from him and put them into the trunk.

"Mom—" He started to argue. How were they in the navy anymore? "It's only because of Dad—"

"Don't," she said. "Please." She took him by the shoulders and looked long and hard into his eyes. "What would I do without you?" she said at last. "I would miss you too much."

They sailed home on a troop ship—navy families, defense workers, and the worst of the wounded men crowded the ship. There were no bands, no banners, and no waving and cheering. The flower ladies were there, as always, selling leis off the backs of their trucks. Adam bought a bunch, and they all wore them.

He stood with his mother and Bea by the railing, the three of them a little apart from the other passengers. His mother held Bea in her arms. Adam thought of Rinaldi and Brown, and the Marine Sergeant, and the officer with his arm in a sling—where were they now? That day had been like a life apart—a whole life lived in that one day—when the war started. He had gone out in the morning riding his bike down the Kamehamema Highway, and he had come home that night carrying a gun.

He looked back at the city as they moved out of the harbor. Beyond Honolulu clouds streamed across the Koolau Mountains like long, fat cigars. His father had smoked cigars sometimes, when he was feeling especially good. Adam liked remembering that, and it hurt him too.

It hurt him to think of his father sealed into that ship. It would always hurt him. People said his father and the other men were heroes who had died at their stations. Heroes who had done amazing things, endured and stood fast. And they had. But when he thought of them down there, when he thought of the way they had died, without a chance even to fight back, it only hurt.

In the distance Honolulu and the beaches flattened out until the island seemed to be just mountains floating over the sea. "It's like a dream," his mother said. "So beautiful and so awful."

As they sailed past Diamond Head, the flat, old volcano, people dropped their leis into the sea. It meant you were coming back. Adam let his lei go and watched it drop into the water. *Goodbye, Dad.*

In the water the flowers formed rafts of color. For a moment the whole sea seemed to glow, and then it faded.

AUTHOR'S NOTE

Pearl Harbor was the worst single naval defeat in American history. The attack was over in less than two hours, but the war that began that day was to continue for nearly four years. Few expected Japan, a small nation with limited resources, to attack a nation as big and powerful as the United States. The Pearl Harbor naval base, the home station of the U.S. Pacific Fleet, was on Oahu, the most populated of the eight Hawaiian islands. It had huge fuel and ammunition depots and was ringed with airfields. One hundred thousand military personnel— army, navy, and marines—were on the Hawaiian islands, whose waters were routinely patrolled by ships and planes. Pearl Harbor was considered impregnable.

The Japanese attack depended on stealth, surprise, and luck. On November 26 the Japanese attack fleet, which had gathered secretly in the fog-shrouded waters of the Kuril Islands of northern Japan, set sail through the heavy seas of the North Pacific. The fleet included six aircraft carriers and two battleships, as well as support cruisers, destroyers, and supply ships. Had they been discovered, they would have turned back, but despite the thousands of miles of water crossed during the next twelve days, the fleet was never detected.

The first of two waves of attacking aircraft was launched at

0600. A Sunday morning was chosen because it was the custom for the Pacific Fleet to be on maneuvers during the week and back in port on the weekend. The Japanese attack force consisted of 360 airplanes, including high-level bombers, torpedo bombers, and dive-bombers, as well as 43 Zero fighter planes. The first bombs struck Ford Island at 0755. At almost the same time, every American airfield around the island was attacked. Within minutes the air defense of Pearl Harbor was nearly destroyed.

When the attack was over, 2,403 American servicemen were dead, nearly half from the *Arizona*, which sank in nine minutes, trapping more than 1,000 men belowdecks. Including the wounded, but not counting civilian losses, the Pearl Harbor casualties totaled almost 3,500. Japan lost fewer than 100 men.

Five U.S. battleships were sunk, and three destroyers and three light cruisers were damaged. Japan lost one full-size submarine and five midget submarines that had been probing the waters around Pearl Harbor. The Japanese fleet itself escaped undetected.

One hundred sixty-four U.S. aircraft were destroyed, almost all on the ground. In addition, one hundred fifty-nine more were badly damaged. Of the twenty-nine Japanese planes that failed to return to their carriers, most were shot down by American antiaircraft guns and the handful of American fighter pilots who managed to get airborne.

Despite the battle's one-sided results, the attack didn't achieve the goal of destroying the U.S. Pacific Fleet and immobilizing the American forces. The Japanese failed to destroy the massive fuel reserves or the naval repair yards at Pearl Harbor, so instead of the Pacific Fleet being forced back to the mainland, the damage was repaired in Hawaii. In addition, Pearl Harbor was so shallow that sunken ships that would have been a total loss in deeper water were eventually refloated. It took several years, but in the end the U.S. Navy recovered all but three vessels. Eighty percent of the aircraft were also salvaged.

More important, the attack was a psychological disaster for Japan. Americans responded with fury to the attack, and "Remember Pearl Harbor" became the rallying cry of the war in the Pacific. The U.S. Navy launched its first attack on Japanese installations less than two months later, and the fleet was on the attack at full strength in six months.

The attack on Pearl Harbor was made more effective because of widespread American racist attitudes toward the Japanese. Simply put, Americans considered themselves superior to the Japanese in every way. The common view was that Japan would never dare attack the U.S., and if it did, the Americans would easily prevail. The American military was less concerned about an air or naval attack from Japan than about sabotage by the Japanese living in Hawaii. At the time of the attack a third of Hawaii's population, 160,000 people, were of Japanese descent—immigrants who had lived and worked in Hawaii for many years but were denied citizenship, and their children who were born in Hawaii and were American citizens.

The military view at the highest levels was that in the event of war, Hawaiian Japanese would side with Japan and interfere with the war effort. To minimize sabotage, the army had ordered all American planes to be lined up wingtip to wingtip so they could be guarded more easily. Under attack they were more easily destroyed. In the days and weeks after the attack rumors of sabotage were common.

On the Pacific coast of the United States the same anti-Japanese hysteria led to mass internments of 110,000 Americans of Japanese ancestry (AJA), most of them American citizens. Citizens or not, on the West Coast families were given a week to dispose of their goods. With numbered tags around their necks, they were packed into trains—the blinds drawn—and sent to ten internment camps in desolate areas, where they lived in prisonlike conditions surrounded by barbed wire and guard towers.

A similar call for the internment of Hawaii's AJA population was raised, but it wasn't feasible to carry out such an order. Americans of Japanese ancestry were too numerous and too important to the economy of Hawaii. Some arrests were made, but they involved fewer than 1 percent of the Hawaiian AJA population.

There was not a single case of sabotage by Japanese citizens during WWII. In fact, many young Americans of Japanese ancestry served valiantly in the defense of the United States. When an all-Hawaiian army unit was formed, more than 9,500 men, all AJAs, volunteered, and the 442nd Regimental Combat Team became the most highly decorated unit in U.S.

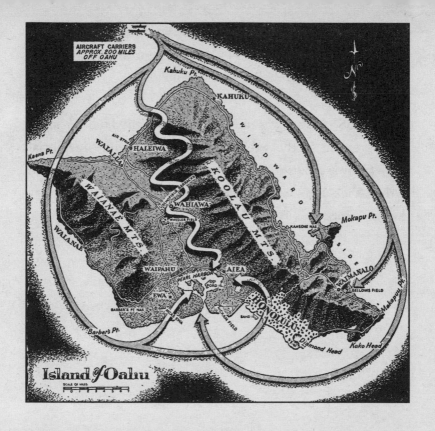

Island of Oahu

SCALE OF MILES

military history. The 442nd fought in Italy and France in some of the fiercest battles of the war. In 1944 the 442nd rescued the Lost Battalion, the 211 survivors of the 141st Army Battalion, a Texas unit surrounded by the Germans. In this operation the 442nd lost 200 men. Six hundred others were wounded, a 60 percent casualty rate.

The racism that poisoned America's attitude toward its Japanese citizens also affected another sector of Americans. African-Americans were restricted in the navy to positions in food service and personal care of officers. But Dorie Miller, a mess attendant on the *West Virginia*, was the first American hero of WWII. He took over machine guns during the Pearl Harbor attack and fought so valiantly that he received the Navy Cross.

The USS *Arizona* was never raised, and the bodies it contained remain in the wreck. Today a long white memorial stands athwart the sunken ship to commemorate all who died in the attack. Droplets of oil still rise from the hulk. Some say they are tears.